Pelekinesis

Codex Ocularis by Ian Pyper

ISBN-10: 1-938349-25-3
ISBN-13: 978-1-938349-25-6
eISBN: 978-1-938349-15-7
Copyright © 2016 Ian Pyper

Artwork and text by Ian Pyper
Layout and Book Design by Mark Givens

First Pelekinesis Printing 2016
For information: Pelekinesis, 112 Harvard Ave #65,
Claremont, CA 91711 USA

www.pelekinesis.com

Codex Ocularis

Ian Pyper

To all those that have gone before—
most notably Robert RN Calvert of the
Société Astronomæ/Captain of the Spaceship
Hawkwind and also Commander John J
Adams of the United Planets Star Cruiser
C-57D and his deep space mission to Altair IV.

Imagination will often carry us to worlds that never were. But without it we go nowhere.

Carl Sagan

Codex Ocularis

This is the observer's log book of solo cybernaut Ian L. Pyper and it details (albeit in abridged, annotated and fragmented form) the exploration out into the darkest depths of deep space.

The chance discovery of a viable and stable wormhole and the subsequent development of cyber holospace technology enabled this mission to be imagined and executed in a relatively short space in time.

The parallel development of the iProbe (TM) series (originally primarily for military use) of virtual reality deep space data transmission drones allowed this mission to develop in unexpected and exciting ways.

Mostly 'fact' and direct scientific observation, although some elements of hallucination and dream may have inadvertently filtered into the descriptive narrative and visual notation. The eye and brain and other senses are often seemingly deceived on many occasions within the virtual environment – particularly when applied to the projection into a distant and alien world such as Planet Ocularis.

Here are the log-book notes and schematic exploration drawings - a journey of discovery into the past, present + future.

A first exploration into the deepest, darkest regions of space. The chance discovery of a viable, stable wormhole and the development of cyber-space virtual reality technology has enabled this mission to Oailaxis to be imagined and executed in a relatively short space in time.

Travelling at the speed of thought - passing through the synapses of the brain, through convoluted passages and pathways and deep real and imagined spaces.

Through thoughts, dreams, visions, notions and ideas - from the brain, the neural stem and the aether - the mind, the consciousness and the subconsciousness - the frontal lobes, the Cerebellum, Cerebrum, Medullary cortex and the spinal chord.

Tracing a journey through virtual space and time or whatever (or wherever....).

Disembodied thoughts and observations becoming tangible and real, but at the back of the mind there is still halluination and the distinct possibility / inevitability of mis-
-reading of information...

This log-book is fragmented and incomplete.
Selected abridged and annotated extracts,
observations and revisions are all that remain.
Most is 'fact', although some elements of
hallucination and dream have potentially
filtered into the attempted descriptive and
visual narrative and notation.

Sometimes it has become
problematic to separate the
visions of 'reality' from those
of illusion in the deceptive
depths of deep space virtual
reality / cyberspace exploration.
Errors will inevitably occur and
the eye, brain and other senses
may be seemingly deceived in
the virtual reality projected
environment of a planet such
as Aularis.

"Initial studies have shown changes in psychological, cognitive and physiological effects - humans are neurophysiologically wired to interpret stimulus and so there is the real danger that the immersed cybernaut may not be able to re-engage with the 'real' world. The human brain may not be able to process the leap into a virtual reality 'alien' environment."

Taken from the official pre-mission medical risk assessment files

The One, the most perfect being 'cannot remain shut up in itself'; it must overflow and create the world of ideas, which in turn creates a copy or image of itself in the universal soul.

Arthur Koestler, 'The Sleepwalkers'

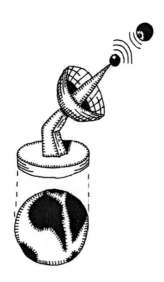

Notes on Diagrams & Projections:

Structures are in graphic styles designed to bring out salient features such as curvature and certain topographic details.

Diagrams compiled from the currently known and measurable data. These diagrams and projections are presented to extrapolate certain elements or concepts connected to Oarlaxis, but no projection or diagrammatical treatment can maintain ALL of the properties of the planet.

NB: Certain diagrams are more accurate than others and have been made in order to give the best possible overview of particular concepts, features and dimensions. True and absolutely accurate representation is impossible within the limitations of this preliminary exploration and can only be fully obtained more accurately in any possible future mission(s).

Distortions and anomalies in the diagrammatic projections are therefore inevitable and unavoidable.

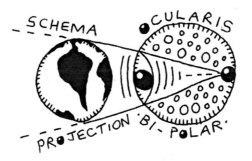

In addition, some aspects of the Ocularis mission have been omitted from the log-book notation and transcripts in an attempt to maintain the secret location of the planet and so protect the delicate balance of the organisms exsisting there.

It was decided that minimal human interference would be recommended so as to allow the continuance of natural evolution and development on the planet uninterrupted.

Therefore, only brief notational schematic star maps have been provided. These codified diagrams are of a general nature only and provided purely for reference and offer no direct and obvious clues as to the exact location and position of Ocularis in relation to adjacent known star systems.

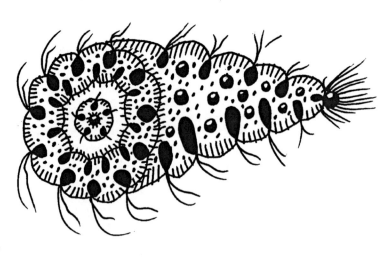

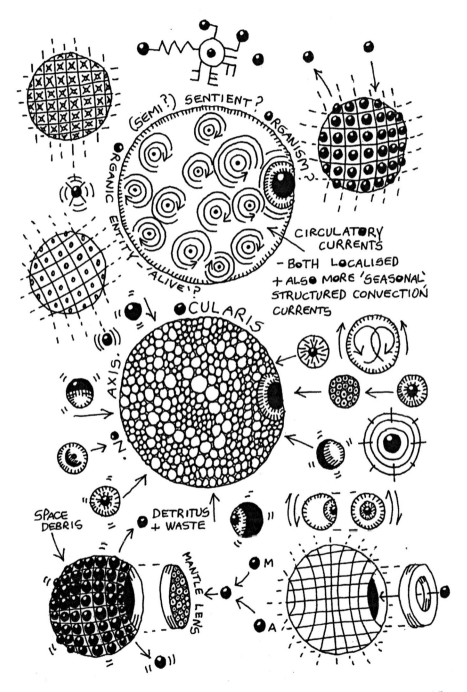

(SEMI?) SENTIENT? ORGANISM?

ORGANIC ENTITY - 'ALIVE'?

CIRCULATORY CURRENTS
- BOTH LOCALISED
+ ALSO MORE 'SEASONAL'
STRUCTURED CONVECTION
CURRENTS

...CULARIS

AXIS.

...N.

SPACE DEBRIS

DETRITUS + WASTE

MANTLE LENS

M

A

15

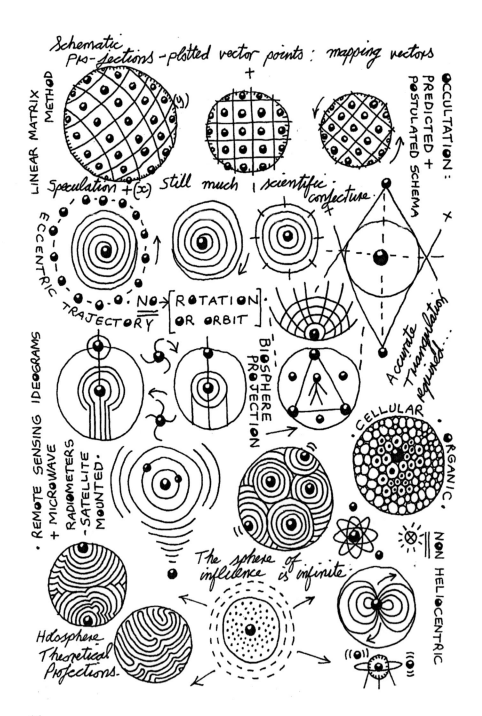

Schematic Pro-jections - plotted vector points : mapping vectors

LINEAR MATRIX METHOD

OCCULTATION : PREDICTED + POSTULATED SCHEMA

Speculation +(x) still much | scientific conjecture

ECCENTRIC TRAJECTORY

NO → [ROTATION OR ORBIT]

Accurate Triangulation required...

BIOSPHERE PROJECTION

CELLULAR

ORGANIC

· REMOTE SENSING IDEOGRAMS + MICROWAVE RADIOMETERS - SATELLITE MOUNTED ·

NON HELIOCENTRIC

The sphere of influence is infinite

Holosphere Theoretical Projections.

'Alchemy' of biological and atomic complexities

A living cosmic body? 'memory'?

VR + Teleport window —
— 'Action-at-a-distance'
— point of entry
— 360° in any direction depending on aperture zone position.

[* DIAGRAM NOTATION ONLY — sizes and distances]
[are still vague and as yet unconfirmed]

Magnetic Gravitational 'observant'

— an obtuse / oblique vision of the universe
— a cosmic paradox?

PAN-OPTIC

Geocentric?
Heliocentric?
↓ Hydrocentric?
obviously some degree of sun-star and Earth focus.
— cosmic 'awareness'.

[*ALGORITHS INDICATE OBJECTS CURVED INTO 4TH DIMENSION + VIBRATIONS BEYOND THE NORMAL POWER OF THE SENSES]

MYSTERIUM COSMOGRAPHICUM
[—'Harmony of the Sphere'.] · Hydro-spherical spatial displacement.

Early findings would indicate that the depth of the world may not be the only prequisite for / of the 'gaze' of Oculoris. As a direct result, variations and abstractions occur with great frequency and opportunity ...

17

The diagram is labeled with the following text:

SPACE DEBRIS + STAR 'DUST' + LOOSE 'FLOATERS' + 'BRAIN' ASTEROID CALCIUM CONCRETIONS

ORBITAL MOONS

BRAIN ASTEROID

COSMIC DUST

BELT

ATMOSPHERE

VAPOUR

INTERNAL OCEAN

CORAL-LIKE CALCIUM CONCRETIONS

COSMIC DUST

COSMIC DUST

The deep ocean trench made mostly of detritus and large calcium coral-like concretions that have developed over the millenia during the unique evolution of Ocularis — comparitively small excess sections apparently break free due to a combination of chemical and internal current forces — these are carried in the strong convection currents and are circulated to the semi-permeable lens mantle and ejected through it - these 'brain' asteroids then remain in orbit around Ocularis, although some occasionally drifts into space.

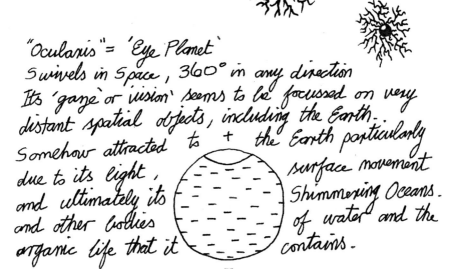

"Ocularis" = 'Eye Planet'
Swivels in Space, 360° in any direction
Its 'gaze' or 'vision' seems to be focussed on very
distant spatial objects, including the Earth.
Somehow attracted to + the Earth particularly
due to its light,   surface movement
and ultimately its   shimmering Oceans.
and other bodies   of water and the
organic life that it   contains.

Its Cyclops-like 'stare' - its vigilant gaze seems
active and yet somehow seemingly passive at
the same time. Almost defiantly gazing out
across the universe in any possible direction.

Immense and almost completely spherical - 'alive'
in a very real sense of the word - a living cosmic
body silently shimmering in the deepest, darkest
regions of space.

Further measurement and observation now needs to
be completed to determine the exact nature of this
mysterious 'watery' astral enigma X million light
years distant from ourselves here on Earth.

Star Map Sequence — Virtual Schematic Projection:

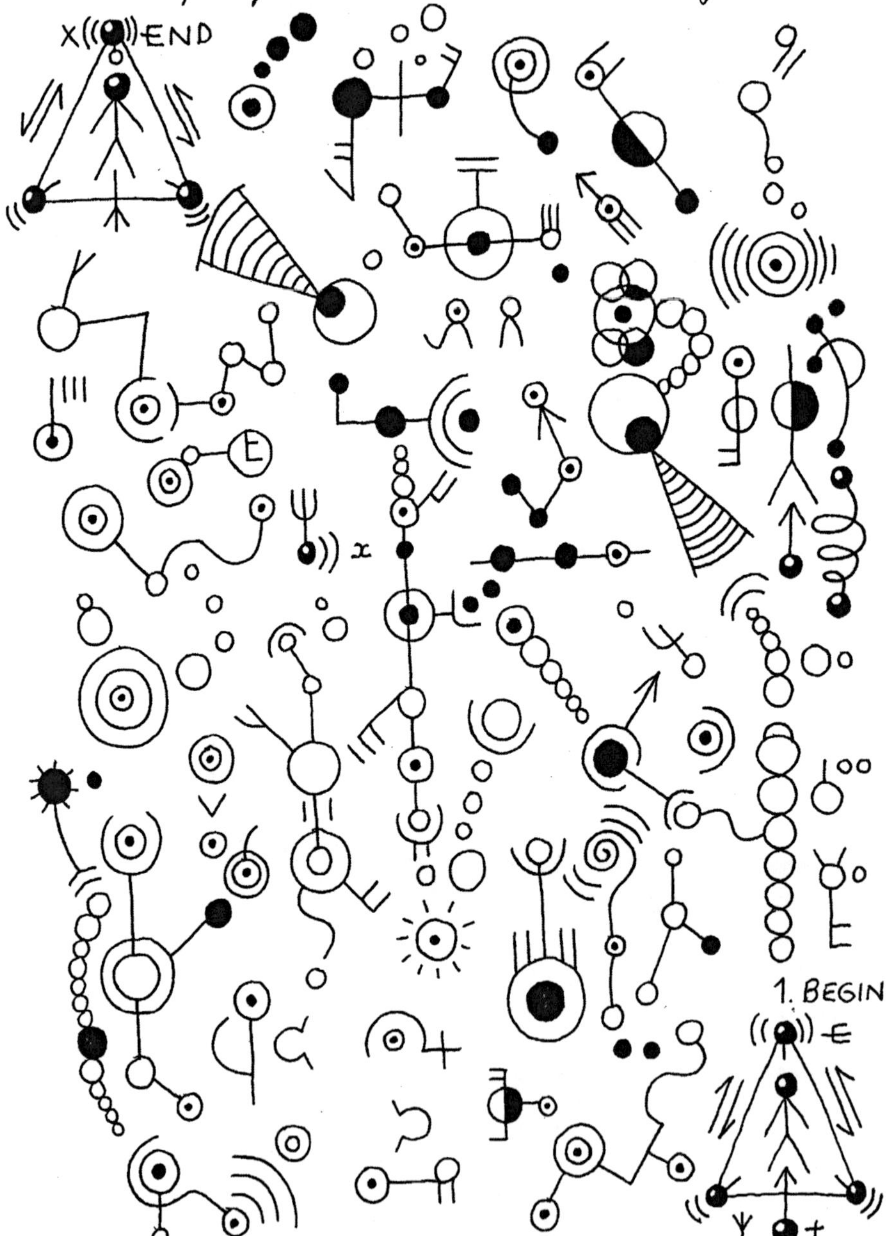

X((●))END

x

1. BEGIN ∈

Υ +

Twin Moons of Planet Ocularis:

The twin moons of Horus and Osiris are
predominantly Calcium Carbonate in a crystalline
form.
Structure is organic/inorganic matrix - nacreous,
iridescent and opalescent.
It would appear that the moons both formed
as 'blisters' within Ocularis and are thought
to be the product of some kind of spontaneous
ejection of accumulated debris. The 'waste'
matter was probably expelled/expunged via
the Iris aperture and subsequently formed
the two contra-rotating orbiting moons.

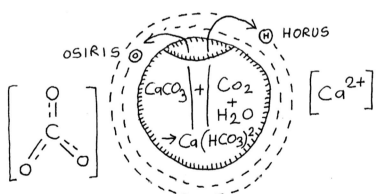

Creates a balanced, stable equilibrium in a
fixed biological system — the 2 moons are
the by-products of this self-regulatory bio-
-sphere.

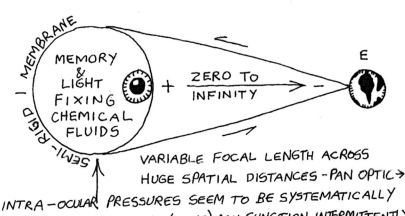

MEMBRANE

SEMI-RIGID

MEMORY & LIGHT FIXING CHEMICAL FLUIDS

+

ZERO TO INFINITY

−

E

VARIABLE FOCAL LENGTH ACROSS
HUGE SPATIAL DISTANCES - PAN OPTIC →

INTRA-OCULAR PRESSURES SEEM TO BE SYSTEMATICALLY
MAKING THE PLANET'S 'LENS' MALFUNCTION INTERMITTENTLY
− SPOILED AND INCOMPLETE / DISTORTED VISUAL DATA
− DEGENERATION AND FIELD LOSS. BLURRING OF DETAIL.
MONOSCOPIC 'VISION' LIMITS DEPTH OF FIELD.
SUBSEQUENT OBTUSE/OBLIQUE VISION AND ZONES OF
DISPLACEMENT AND A DEPTH OF FIELD CRISIS OF OPTICAL
DENSITY. DESCRIBED AS 'POETIC' VISION.

OCCUPYING A SPACE ON THE EDGES OF THE OBSERVABLE
UNIVERSE AND IN SEMI-OCCULTATION AND INTERMITTENTLY
OBSCURED BY PLANETARY BODIES, LIGHT POLLUTION AND
SPACE DEBRIS AND DUST.

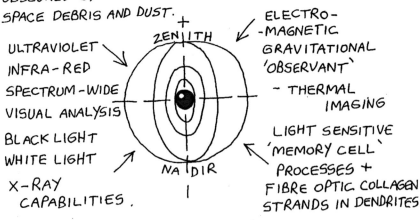

+

ZENITH

ULTRAVIOLET
INFRA-RED
SPECTRUM-WIDE
VISUAL ANALYSIS

BLACK LIGHT
WHITE LIGHT

X-RAY
CAPABILITIES.

NADIR

ELECTRO-
-MAGNETIC
GRAVITATIONAL
'OBSERVANT'

− THERMAL
IMAGING

LIGHT SENSITIVE
'MEMORY CELL'
PROCESSES +
FIBRE OPTIC COLLAGEN
STRANDS IN DENDRITES

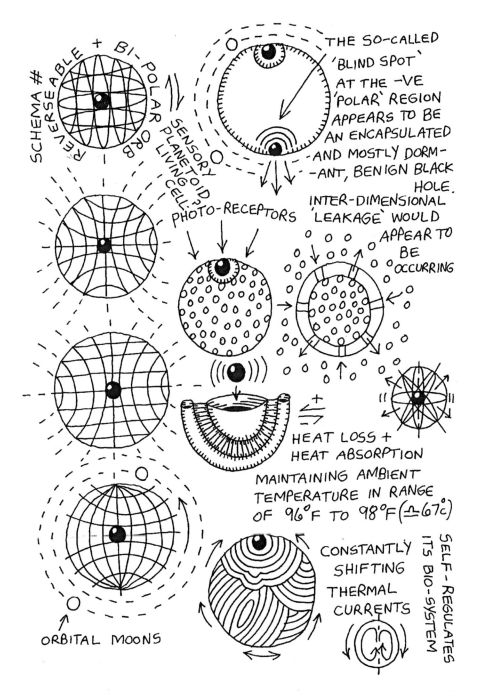

OSMOTIC COVERING MEMBRANE - CELLULAR + SEMI-PERMEABLE

LIGHT

LENS

MANTLE

'AQUEOUS' REGION BIOSPHERE 'SEA OF MEMORY'

PROTO-GALAXY 'PYP - 1 - 55a'

LIGHT, COSMIC DEBRIS & GAS ABSORPTION

ATMOSPHERE + ELECTRICAL MAGNETIC FIELD

A 'living' planet - cyclops-like. Defiantly gazing out across the universe in any direction.

360° PLANETARY SHIFT IN ALL DIRECTIONS

ōkyələrāis o·ku·la·ri·s

Almost like the 'Eye of God' - a blink in the mind of the Cosmos ?! Maybe the 'discriminating eye' of consciousness?

LIGHT FROM DISTANT SUNS

EARTH

Photo-tonic Infra-Red

ultraviolet + visible light spectrum - 'Black' light - Electromagnetic sensory capability - Thermal imaging Ocularis appears to act as some kind of discriminating 'Space Brain' ('Meme' Brain ?) and spontaneously create living organisms within its aqueous 'miasma'. Focussed on the Earth, the 'eye' of Ocularis seems to create life mimicking certain organisms from our world.

CELL BODY - 'OCULARIS'
LIVING PLANETARY

'Cosmosis' = Ions and Proteins
- molecules and atoms — ?
permeable to non-polar and/or
hydrophobic molecules - travel
through the plasma membrane.

Pressure of 'cell' is largely
maintained by (c)osmosis
across 'the cell' membrane between the interior
and its relatively hypotonic environment.

Cosmotic spontaneous net movement of solvent
ions and molecules through partially permeable
membranes into a higher solute concentration
region.

MOLECULES
=
IONS
KINETIC
ENERGY
CELL
BODY

Self-contained, mutualist, non-parasitic bio-
-system — harmonious and self-balancing and
self-regulating communal eco-system.
The perfect utopian, benign biosphere?

SCHEMA # 2

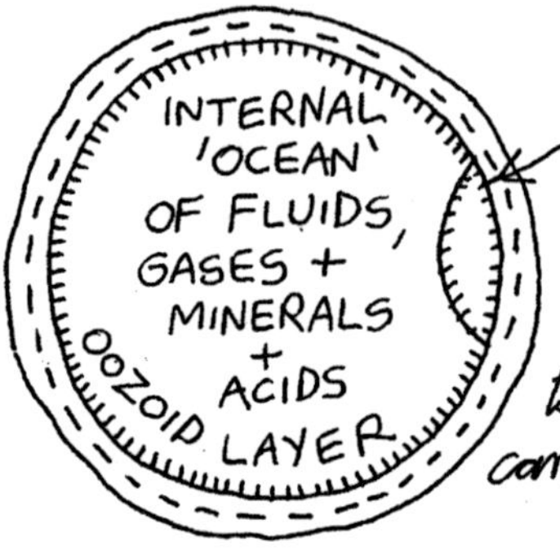

INTERNAL
'OCEAN'
OF FLUIDS,
GASES +
MINERALS
+
ACIDS
OOZOID LAYER

PLASMA (PLASMOID)
IRIS MANTLE

Ocularis would appear
to have a form of what
can only be described as
'Astral Astigmatism'

The ability of Ocularis to create life mimicking
that of organic life on Earth is subsequently
flawed and errors have obviously developed over
the millenia and scale and reproduction of
the mimicked organisms contain what only can
be described as 'poetic' errors.

The memory-fixing chemical fluids present within
the 'aqueous' regions of the planet enable Ocularis
somehow to spontaneously generate new life,
albeit in a mutated and evolved form. Almost
like an alchemy of atomic, molecular and
organic complexity.

The intra-ocular pressures would seem to be
responsible for a slight lens dysfunctionality and
as a direct result a loss in clarity of focus, field
loss, 'macular' degeneration and spoiled and incomplete
visual data. Monoscopic/Monocular 'gaze' also seems
to limit depth of field and blurring and distortion,
parallax and loss of detail.

"Swimming in an 'ocean' gene Pool"

NEURAL NETWORK INTERCONNECTIONS

The complexities of spontaneous creation and growth and development. From molecules and microbes to molluscs — from the single cell to the complexities of cell communities. Micro and Macro become interchangeable in the Oceanic streams of consciousness . . . .

A subconscious 'sea of memory' - a psy-planet, the globe-eye living organic space-brain.
Streams of consciousness arising from the darkest depths and a possibly primitive proto-mind.
Something dredged up from the ooze of a remote and prehistoric past or something pointing towards a possible future?
Primal chaos growing from the darkness and refining slowly into form, flesh and bone - a slow process of evolution. Proto-embryonic evolutionary in their development . . . . . will these creatures eventually develop backbones?

All growing and developing in a cosmic laboratory of gelatinous plasma, amino acids, electrolytes, acids, globular proteins and in a viscosity higher than that of oceanic salt water.

27

SCHEMA # 3

GELATINOUS PLASMA,
LOW PROTEIN SECRETIONS,
AMINO ACIDS,
ELECTROLYTES.

GLOBULAR
     PROTEINS,
SODIUM, CALCIUM,
POTASSIUM,
CHLORIDES
– HIGH H_2O
CONCENTRATION
SALTS, SUGARS
TRACE ELEMENTS
          +
BACTERIAL OXIDATIVE
PROCESSES AND
OXIDATION (OXIDISATION
OF NITRATES INTO
          NITRITES)
HUMUS, NITROGEN,
NATURAL DECAY,
AMMONIUM COMPOUNDS,
NUTRIENTS & MINERALS

VISIBLE
LIGHT SPECTRUM + 'LOOSE'
          PHOTONS
     PHOTONIC
COSMIC DUST,
     PHOTOSYNTH-
     -ESIS   SPACE
               DEBRIS

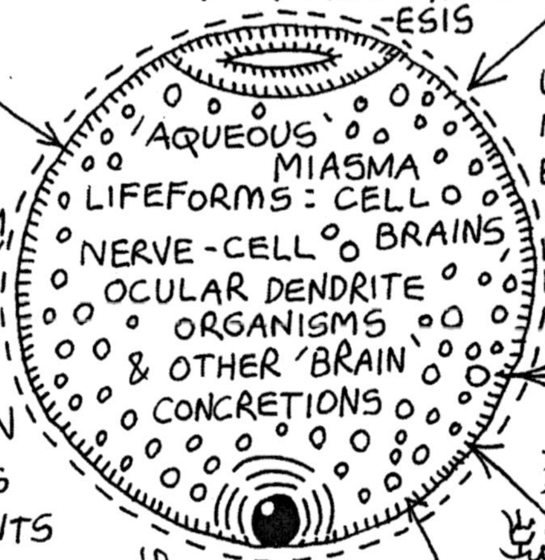

AQUEOUS
     MIASMA
LIFEFORMS: CELL
NERVE-CELL BRAINS,
OCULAR DENDRITE
ORGANISMS
& OTHER 'BRAIN'
CONCRETIONS

ULTRAVIOLET,
INFRA-RED,
ELECTRO –
-MAGNETIC
X-RAYS,
BLACK LIGHT

— PHOTO-
-RECEPTORS

SINGULARITY

OOZE

SEMI-DORMANT
BLACK HOLE
(BENIGN ?)
CONTAINED
IN STASIS

MUTUALIST,
SYMBIOTIC
+ NON-
PARASITIC

ORGANIC
     LIFEFORMS
'EYE' NUCLEI
- ALMOST LIKE
NEURAL NETWORKS
-INTERCONNECTED
AND EVOLVING.
— CELL COMMUNITIES.

MIMETICAL ORGANISMS
-SPONTANEOUSLY DEVELOPING.
THE MICROSCOPIC BECOMES
THE MACROSCOPIC (AND VICE VERSA) - PREDOMINANTLY
AQUATIC (ALMOST EXCLUSIVELY?) IN NATURE - HYBRID
SOFT-BODIED MOLLUSC AND INVERTERBRATE AND SOME
VAGUE REPLICATION OF CERTAIN HUMANOID CHARACTER-
-ISTICS - MOSTLY SOFT-BONED AND LACKING IN KERATIN
FIBROUS STRUCTURAL PROTEINS. COMPLEX AND YET
                    INCOMPLETE.

COSMOSIS = ions + proteins permeable to non-polar and/or hydrophobic molecules - travel through the plasma membrane. Pressure of the 'cell' is largely maintained by cosmosis across the 'cell' membrane between the interior and its relatively hypotonic environment.

BIOSPHERE

SPACE DUST + DEBRIS ABSORPTION (METEORS, COMETS + OTHER ROCK FRAGMENTS)

ABSORPTION OF LIGHT- VISIBLE SPECTRUM/ INFRA-RED, ULTRA-VIOLET + BLACK LIGHT

COSMIC RADIATION + GASES

SEMI-PERMEABLE MEMBRANE

Cosmotic spontaneous net movement of solvent ions + molecules through partially permeable membrane into a region of higher solute concentration.

IONS
PLANET 'CELL'
MOLECULES

KINETIC ENERGY

Biological membrane → Biological systems - A living 'cell'? A self regulating system.

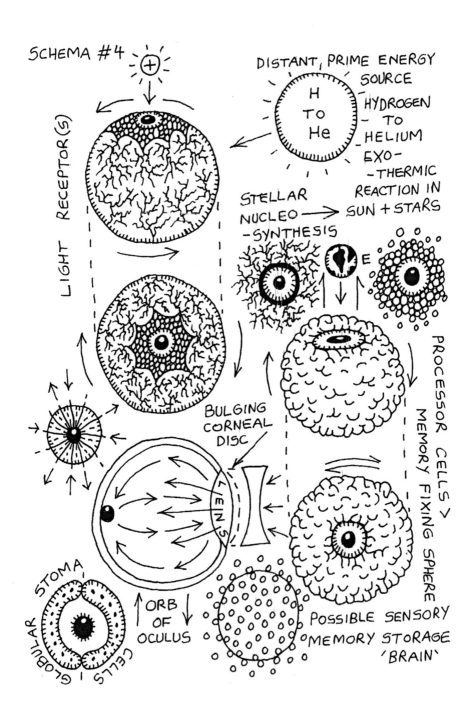

SCHEMA #4

DISTANT, PRIME ENERGY SOURCE

H TO He

HYDROGEN TO HELIUM EXO- -THERMIC REACTION IN SUN + STARS

STELLAR NUCLEO -SYNTHESIS

LIGHT RECEPTOR(S)

PROCESSOR CELLS > MEMORY FIXING SPHERE

BULGING CORNEAL DISC

L E N S

GLOBULAR STOMA CELLS

ORB OF OCULUS

POSSIBLE SENSORY MEMORY STORAGE 'BRAIN'

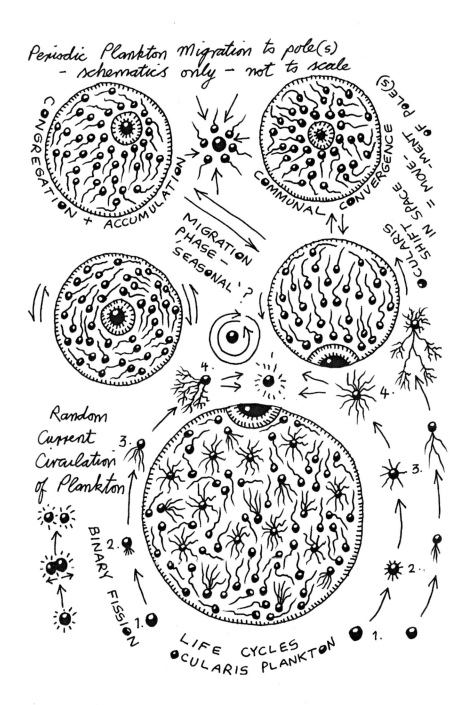

Periodic Plankton migration to pole(s)
— schematics only — not to scale

CONGREGATION + ACCUMULATION

COMMUNAL CONVERGENCE

OCULARIS SHIFT IN SPACE = MOVE-MENT OF POLE(S)

MIGRATION PHASE — SEASONAL '?

Random Current Circulation of Plankton

BINARY FISSION

4.

1.

4.

3.

3.

2.

2.

1.

1.

LIFE CYCLES
OCULARIS PLANKTON

31

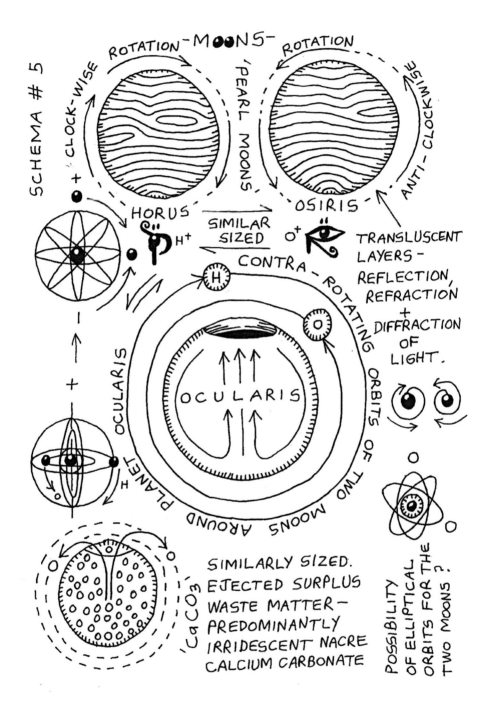

SCHEMA # 5

ROTATION —MOONS— ROTATION

+ CLOCK-WISE

ANTI-CLOCKWISE

'PEARL MOONS'

HORUS

OSIRIS

H^+

SIMILAR SIZED

O^+

CONTRA-ROTATING ORBITS OF TWO MOONS AROUND PLANET

TRANSLUSCENT LAYERS — REFLECTION, REFRACTION + DIFFRACTION OF LIGHT.

H

O

OCULARIS

−

+

'CaCO₃'

SIMILARLY SIZED. EJECTED SURPLUS WASTE MATTER — PREDOMINANTLY IRRIDESCENT NACRE CALCIUM CARBONATE

POSSIBILITY OF ELLIPTICAL ORBITS FOR THE TWO MOONS ?

The planetary habitability and lifeforms are obviously extrapolations of those on Earth. Astrobiology, Geophysical, Geochemical and astrophysical criteria obviously apply, just more research is required.

Some Earth-like ocean chemistry similarities
- complex organic molecules and cellular organisms
- the cell-brain soma main body of Ocularis has no fixed centre and is a nerve matrix of organic lifeforms.

Ocularis would appear to be sentient/semi-sentient (saprient/semi sapient)

SPHEROID

Metabolic processes + gaseous exchange. Layered skin - some form of Plasma/Protoplasma fluid within the planet membrane(s)

A magnetic field + gravitational field create the contain-ment field for the fluid giant hydrosphere.

There appears to be some cellular mimetic memory within the amorphous organic matrix and there seems to be an exact balance in generation, re-generation and decay - a pure ecosystem. No direct communication with either Ocularis or its lifeforms has yet been attempted

The 'brain' of Ocularis absorbs mimetic memories, albeit imperfect ones - an active, interconnected dynamic nerve matrix - abstract cognition in space?

Is the planet sentient?

Observations would indicate that the ability of Oculanis to refocus its 'gaze' in space and for it to have an active interaction between itself and its greater environment would suggest sentience.

The interconnectedness of the individual lifeforms and their interaction with one another on some electrical and telepathic level would suggest that there are currents of consciousness that have evolved out of the id-like primal water depths.

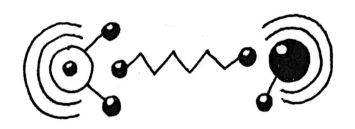

From the subtlest of potential beginnings – a universal manifestation of primal matter clustered in vapour gas clouds and cosmic dust and debris – – slowly spinning in a rotation of light and heat and growing into a spherical object of unique beauty and form.

A living cosmic body – alive in its completeness – a mysterious enigma floating in the distant depths of previously uncharted space.

The Planet Ocularis may, in fact be the eye in which the beauty of the cosmos is reflected. – the harmony of the sphere of the sphere in a unifying vision and luminous synthesis.

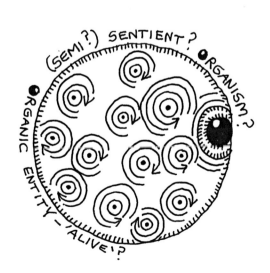

From the depths of the abyss and the underlying void of nothingness came matter in its most embryonic form. In the mysterious depths of the deep, dark trenches, grooves and furrows of the primitive ocean of the mind and flowing in the stream of consciousness, strange and wonderful creatures evolved and moved towards the light.....

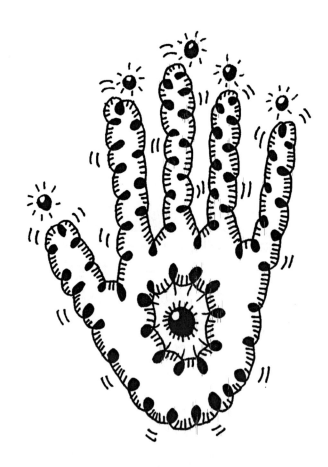

and Sanson-Flamsteed's Sinusoidal, also equal area, can be used for mapping larger areas. Sanson-Flamsteed's projection is particularly suitable for areas across the Equator, ████████ ████ ; Lambert's Equivalent Azimuthal could be used for all the continents or even the world in hemispheres.
For the world, however, none of these projections would be suitable and hence Mollweide and Mercator projections are used, with Zenithal and Oblique Azimuthal Equidistant projections for hemispheres.
+OCULARIS:
Projections used in the atlas are as follows:
Conical (scale correct along meridians and standard parallel) pp. 34, 35.
Conical with two standard parallels (scale correct along meridians and both standard parallels) pp. xiv, xv, xxii, xxiii, 6, 7, 8, 9, 10, 11, 12, 13, 14, 15, 16, 17, 18, 19, 20, 21, 22, 23, 24, 30, 31, 32, 33, 46, 47.

Bonne (Equal Area) pp. xii, xiii, xviii, xix, xxiv, 4, 5, 28, 29, 37, 40, 41, 42, 43, 44, 45, 58, 59, 60, 61, 76.
Conical Orthomorphic with two standard parallels (Correct Shape) 26, 27. Bi-polar oblique Conical Orthomorphic pp. 74, 75.
Lambert's Equivalent Azimuthal (Equal Area) pp. xvi, xvii, xx, xxi, 36, 38, 39, 52, 53, 56, 57, 62, 63, 64, 65.
Sanson-Flamsteed's Sinusoidal (Equal Area) pp. 48, 49, 50, 51, 54, 55, 77, 78, 79.
Alber's Equal Area with two standard parallels pp. 25, 66, 67, 68, 69, 70, 71, 72, 73.
Zenithal Equidistant (distances and bearings are correct from centre) p. 80.
Oblique Azimuthal Equidistant (distances and bearings are correct from centre) pp. 2, 3.
Mercator (True Direction) p. 1.

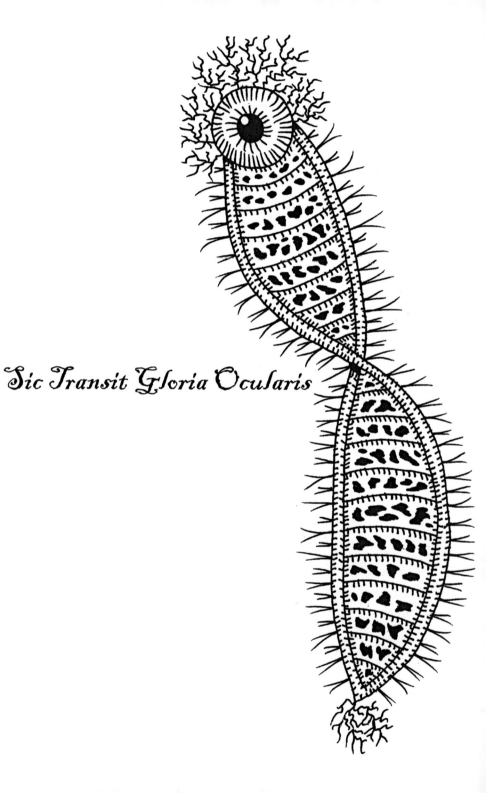

Sic Transit Gloria Ocularis

'There they go off to Mars, just for the ride,

thinking that they will find a planet like a

seer's crystal in which to read a miraculous

future. What they'll find, instead, is a

somewhat shopworn image of themselves.

Mars is a mirror, not a crystal.'

Ray Bradbury, 'The Martian Chronicles'

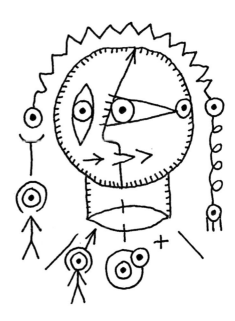

Some aspects of this mission have been omitted and are not currently for full public disclosure due to the delicate environmental balance on Planet Ocularis.

Minimal Human interference is recommended to allow the continued natural evolution and development of the planet and its lifeforms.

Therefore, exact computational data, locations and the proximity to mapped star systems and constellations have been removed.

Certain personal schematic, pictographic, codified and cryptographic notation has been included although these are for visual interest and purely for oblique reference only and offer no direct and obvious clues as to the exact location of Ocularis in relation to adjacent known planetary bodies, star systems or galaxies.

Due to subsequent navigational difficulties, some of the recorded, written data remains erratic, erroneous and incomplete.

Also, some findings, log-book entries, explanations and observations, statements and schematics have been censored and removed to protect the security of the mission to Ocularis.

As the internet of things advances, the very notion of a clear dividing line between reality and virtual reality becomes blurred, sometimes in creative ways.

Geoff Mulgan, Chief Executive, NESTA

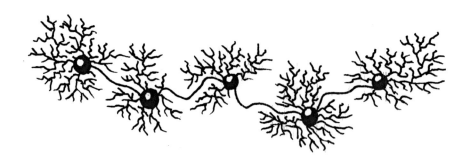

Rough log / Scrap log – preliminary draft.
Smooth log / official log :

<u>NB</u> – Alterations or corrections
the official log-book must be
initialled by the authorised
keeper of the log.

An electronic computer-based log
will be used for the more complex
machine-based components

of the mission.

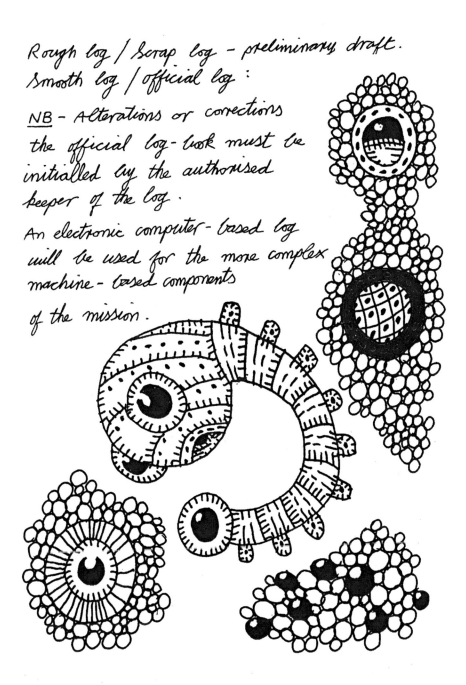

The best simulator for spacewalking is underwater - it allows full visuals and body movement in 3D.

Virtual reality is good too, and has some advantages like full Station simulation, not just part. Like all simulators they have parts that are wrong and misleading: an important thing to remember when preparing for reality.

Chris Hadfield, Astronaut

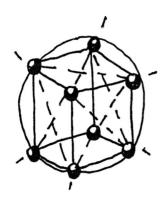

Prime Mission Parameters:

Initial systems calibrations - verification of cyber delivery systems capabilities + performance.

Also, during this extended pilot mission, fact--finding reconnaisance and exploration.
A brief to observe the immediate environment and organisms / lifeforms and to measure and document data.
This is the proverbial 'Quantum Leap' into the unknown. . . .

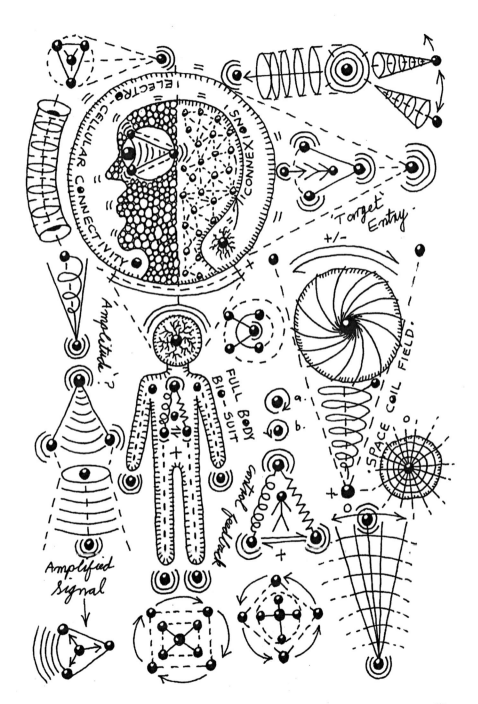

ELECTRO-CELLULAR CONNECTIVITY

CONNEXIONS

'Target' Entry

+/-

Amplitude'?

Amplified signal

FULL BODY BIO-SUIT

Sensor feedback

SPACE COIL FIELD.

a.

b.

47

Planetary implantation data probe the iProbe. Data reconaissance probe (civilian variant) and virtual projection network module. Exploration radar, imaging sensors, frequency receivers, telemetry sensors and full optical, infra-red and ultraviolet sensors, including polarmetric capabilities. Optimised potential for moving & static observation and analysis.

Forms triangulation data receiver in configuration with other iProbes — — outstanding operational range — operational in a wide range of climatic + environmental conditions.

DATA TRANSMISSION STATION (UNMANNED). PLATFORM.

20' / ± 6·096 m

© ASTRODYNE TM

'EXTENDABLE LEGS'

— SELF-RIGHTING + SUBMERSIBLE IN HIGH PRESSURE ENVIRONMENTS

5' ± 1·524 m

'iProbe C2 and variant C3A'

HOME STATION

RECEIVING STATION

+

VARIABLE ORIENTATION

NB: Greater transmission contaimment + stability can be achieved with greater numbers of iProbes in 4 and 5 module configurations, although the triangulation mode is the standard used.

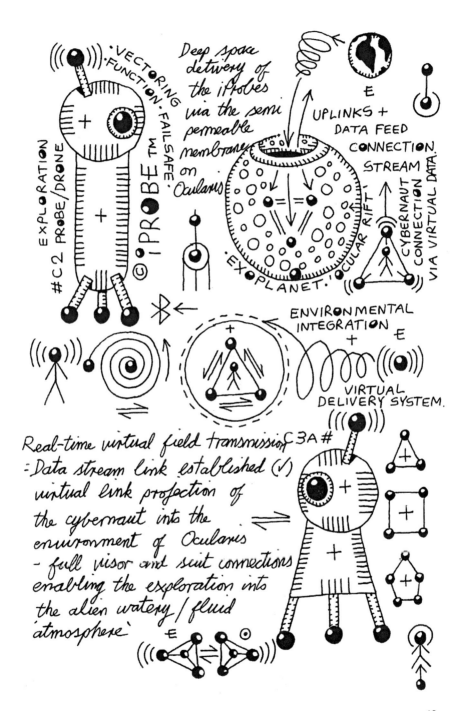

ANCILLARY
SUPPORT (((•)))
FUNCTION:
ILLUMINATION

i Probe supplemental: satellite
support drone - light
source
- focusable
beam
(lux
engine)

Proteus
Xplorer
Deep-sea Light
Tech-nology, LIGHT EMITTER
LUMINOUS POWER LIGHT SUPPORT

Focus
control
[INFINITE]
BEAM
ANGLES

39,000 Flux @ 1 metre
(High and low power
modes).
Powerful search beam
- searchlight — (full battery)
capacity. support.)

BIOSPHERE COMPATIBLE ✓

supplementary
light meters +
photocells

photoscopic vision
+ (light)
scotopic vision
*SPECTRUM (dark)
ADJUSTMENT CAPABILITY.

300 metre depth rated
(3 phase full / half / off) -
+ Full focus control
(Tight to
Flood)
mesopic vision
- between limits and
fully calibrated for spectral
response

Power: Batteries + Radioisotope (RTG)
+ Thermoelectric Generator
Fuel Cell ·☉=☀· (Radioactive Material -
- stores power in - Plutonium)
form of separated Encased in steel sealed shell
Oxygen and Hydrogen - generates heat and
- A thin membrane eventually decays into
between the 2 elements non-radioactive material.
harnesses energy when - Thermocouple Array -
the O and H combine to form H_2O Water.

iProbe Rover Module
'Roving Eye' mode

- Light source mobility capability.

ROVER MODULE

Additional light emitter array 'probe/drone'

FOCUS TO WIDE BEAM

UMBILICAL RELEASE

Supplemental iProbe variants can also be deployed in subsequent missions - 1, 2 or 3 configurations can be applied, allowing greater light penetration and also to stabalise the virtual field of operation.

HEAT EXCHANGE

BIOSPHERE

EXPANDED CONFIGURATION

Certain frequencies of light disappear and others are distorted in aspects of the visual spectrum, therefore additional high power illumination may be required within the VR field of operation. The Roving Eye rover module option will enable greater flexibility and a greater area of exploration.

(*) A camouflage option is also under consideration to allow a much better integration and 'blend in' with the environment of Oculaxis.

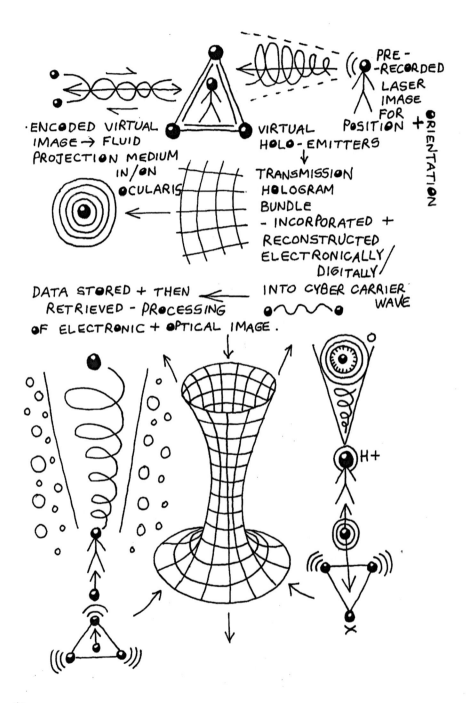

·ENCODED VIRTUAL IMAGE → FLUID PROJECTION MEDIUM IN/ON OCULARIS

VIRTUAL HOLO-EMITTERS
↓
TRANSMISSION HOLOGRAM BUNDLE - INCORPORATED + RECONSTRUCTED ELECTRONICALLY/ DIGITALLY/ INTO CYBER CARRIER WAVE

PRE--RECORDED LASER IMAGE FOR POSITION + ORIENTATION

DATA STORED + THEN RETRIEVED - PROCESSING OF ELECTRONIC + OPTICAL IMAGE.

H+

X

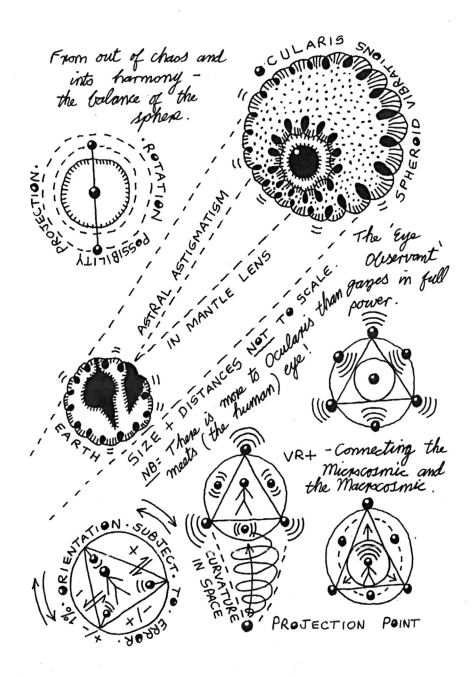

From out of chaos and into harmony — the balance of the sphere.

PROJECTION.

ROTATION POSSIBILITY.

OCULARIS VIBRATIONS SPHEROID

ASTRAL ASTIGMATISM IN MANTLE LENS

EARTH

SIZE + DISTANCES NOT TO SCALE.

NB: There is more to Ocularis than meets (the human) eye!

The 'Eye Observant' gazes in full power.

VR+ - Connecting the Microscomic and the Macrocosmic.

ORIENTATION · SUBJECT · TO · ERROR · +/- %

+
−
+/−
+

CURVATURE IN SPACE

PROJECTION POINT

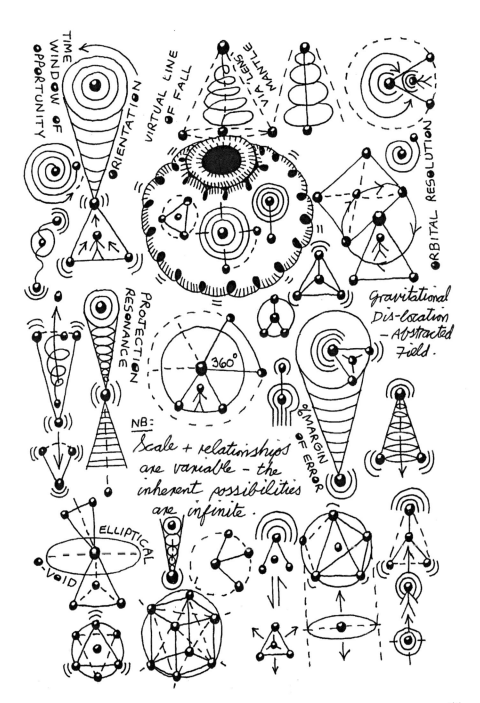

TIME WINDOW OF OPPORTUNITY

ORIENTATION

VIRTUAL LINE OF FALL

VIA LENS / MANTLE

ORBITAL RESOLUTION

PROJECTION RESONANCE

360°

Gravitational Dis-location
- Abstracted Field.

% MARGIN OF ERROR

NB:
Scale + relationships
are variable — the
inherent possibilities
are infinite.

ELLIPTICAL

VOID

55

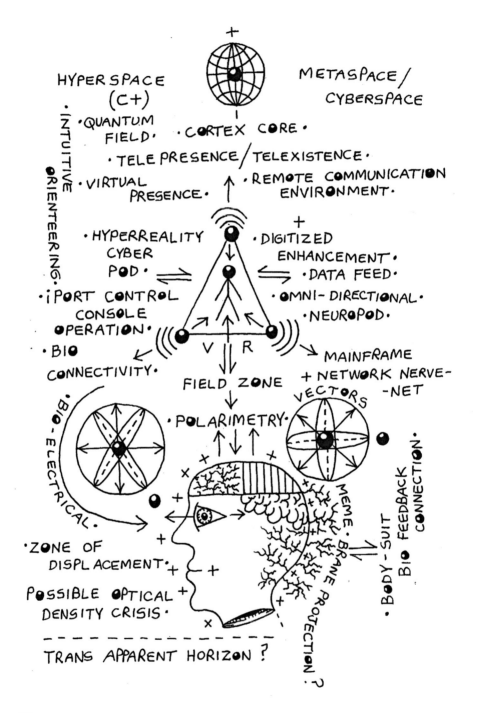

HYPER SPACE (C+)

METASPACE / CYBERSPACE

·INTUITIVE ORIENTEERING·

·QUANTUM FIELD·

·CORTEX CORE·

·TELE PRESENCE / TELEXISTENCE·

·VIRTUAL PRESENCE·

·REMOTE COMMUNICATION ENVIRONMENT·

+

·HYPERREALITY CYBER POD·

·DIGITIZED ENHANCEMENT·

·DATA FEED·

·¡PORT CONTROL CONSOLE OPERATION·

·OMNI-DIRECTIONAL·

·NEUROPOD·

·BIO CONNECTIVITY·

V   R

MAINFRAME + NETWORK NERVE--NET

FIELD ZONE

·POLARIMETRY·

VECTORS

·BIO-ELECTRICAL·

·ZONE OF DISPLACEMENT·

POSSIBLE OPTICAL DENSITY CRISIS·

MEME·BRANE PROJECTION?

·BODY-SUIT BIO FEEDBACK CONNECTION·

TRANS APPARENT HORIZON?

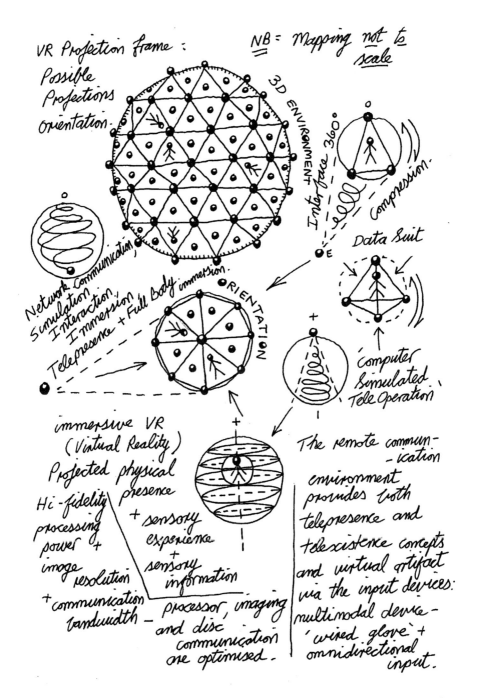

VR Projection frame:
Possible
Projections
orientation.

NB = Mapping not to scale

3D ENVIRONMENT

Interface 360°

Compression.

Network communication.
Simulation.
Interaction.
Immersion
Telepresence + Full Body immersion.

ORIENTATION

Data Suit

Computer
Simulated
Tele Operation

immersive VR
(Virtual Reality)
Projected physical
presence
Hi-fidelity
processing
power +
image
resolution
+ communication
bandwidth −

+ sensory
experience
+
sensory
information

processor, imaging
and disc
communication
are optimised.

The remote commun-
-ication
environment
provides both
telepresence and
telexistence concepts
and virtual artifact
via the input devices:
multimodal device -
'wired glove' +
omnidirectional
input.

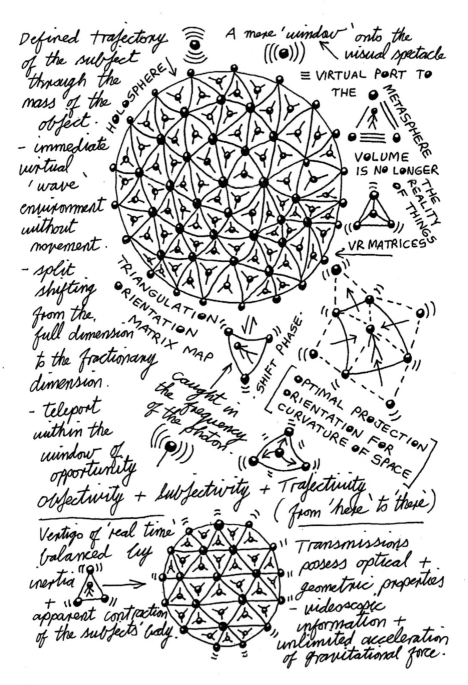

Defined trajectory of the subject through the mass of the object.
- immediate virtual 'wave' environment without movement.
- split shifting from the full dimension to the fractionary dimension.
- teleport within the window of opportunity

A mere 'window' onto the visual spectacle

$\equiv$ VIRTUAL PORT TO THE METASPHERE

$\equiv$ THE REALITY OF THINGS

VOLUME IS NO LONGER

VR MATRICES

HOLOSPHERE

TRIANGULATION ORIENTATION MATRIX MAP

SHIFT PHASE

Caught in the frequency of the photon.

OPTIMAL PROJECTION ORIENTATION FOR CURVATURE OF SPACE

Objectivity + Subjectivity + Trajectivity (from 'here' to 'there')

Vertigo of 'real time' balanced by inertia + apparent contraction of the subjects' body.

Transmissions possess optical + geometric properties
- videoscopic information + unlimited acceleration of gravitational force.

58

unit Quaternions
(versors)
- Using
Euclidean
Rotations
(in three
dimensions)
- LONGITUD -
-INAL
- LATITUDINAL
+
TRANSVERSE
ROTATION

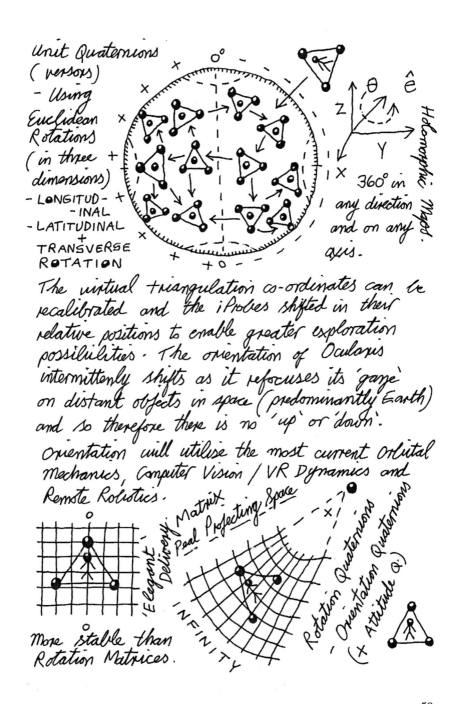

360° in
any direction
and on any
axis.

Holomorphic Maps.

The virtual triangulation co-ordinates can be
recalibrated and the iProbes shifted in their
relative positions to enable greater exploration
possibilities. The orientation of Oculoris
intermittenly shifts as it refocuses its 'gaze'
on distant objects in space (predominantly Earth)
and so therefore there is no 'up' or 'down'.

Orientation will utilise the most current orbital
mechanics, Computer Vision / VR Dynamics and
Remote Robotics.

'Elegant' Delivery Matrix.
Real Projecting Space
INFINITY

Rotation Quaternions
- Orientation Quaternions
(× Attitude Q.)

More stable than
Rotation Matrices.

This rambling and sometimes repetetive and fragmented, non-linear, disjointed and disrupted notes (with some disregard for chronological order!) .... perhaps just trying to mimic the structure and recall of human cognitive function and memory in space-time?

Ultimately it may ~~~~ all only be the disturbed + dysfunctional nature of the virtual connection!

AZIMUTH PROJECTOR CORTEX

CONNECTED WITH THE SENSORY PERCEPTION MESH...

CRANIAL ELECTRO-STIMULATION

REFLUX CAPACITOR

Virtual Projection via Wormhole Hyperspace:

Using current technology, an expedition to Ocularis using rocket technology would prove problematic .... and even impossible.

The chance discovery of the stable wormhole has enabled a whole new set of possibilites - the development of the iProbe programme and the accompanying Virtual cyber suit has made planetary exploration a reality. The advance deployment of the iProbes via the open wormhole and the subsequent virtual projection of the cybernaut into the environment of Ocularis prevents any physical danger to the cybernaut. The cyber link enables safe and secure transport projection. Bio feedback, sensory enhancement and the mind-machine neural activity enhancement technology enables the cybernaut to fully experience and interact with the environment on the /in the planet.

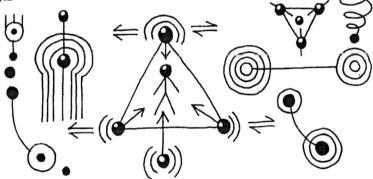

The prototype virtual reality cyber suit (designated 'the Mumia' with some dark sense of humour after the ancient Egyptian burial configuration) and the isolation/flotation 'SARCOPHAGUS' pod ('Sarcophagus) have both wi-fi ISOLATION and hard-wire connections. The pod is soundproofed and the cybernaut in his suit is contained in a very low-light environment.

FLOTATION POD

DATA FEED +

The saline solution in the pod is maintained at an even human body temperature (+/- one degree)

'MUMIA' VIRTUAL REALITY CYBER-SUIT (BIO-ELECTRIC)

COMPUTER MONITORING SYSTEMS + FEEDBACK CONTROL +

DIM BACKGROUND LIGHTING + TEMPERATURE CONTROL

UMBILICAL CONNECTION

The cybernaut experiences a feeling of weightlessness so as to reproduce/replicate the environment on Ocularis.

Each exploration session is limited wherever possible depending on operational requirements and requests for specific data or experiments. Extended periods in the virtual reality environment may result in mental deterioration and also reduced motor functions...

The PROS + CONS of Virtual Reality Space Exploration:

CONS: Short-term intensified isolation + claustrophobia, limited mobility, fatigue + falling levels of concentration.

Psychosis (Paranoid delusions) that may eventually lead to psychiatric disorders. Reality sensory deprivation could make re-adjustment problematic. Prolonged immersion in the body suit + flotation tank may likely result in lower personal performance and possible sensory overload. Altered states of perception and cognisance possibly could result in permanent mental disfunction......

E! Faulty Source Monitoring 'memory' Reflex

PROS: . No Cosmic Radiation.

- No Space sickness.
- No detrimental
- Effects of Weightlessness.
- No Cosmic Radiation.
- No compromised immune system.
- No changes to Blood cells.
- No changes to bone structure.
- No muscle loss.

mission requirements : co-ordinate operation in the following areas : systems, planning, consumables, useage, experiment and 'payload' operations — mission objectives and supporting and remote systems operation. Knowledge of operational characteristics. Safeguards have been put in place to reduce the possibility of 'mission creep'.

Height — 62" – 75" (58.5" × 76" VARIATION)

COGNITIVE SKILLS.

Blood Pressure : = 140/90 (measured in a sitting position)

Hearing : 20 – 20,000 Hz in Audiometric assessment.

Visual acuity : 20/100 or better uncorrected. 20/20 to each eye, although visor headset full compensatory vision software is also present to correct any anomolies. 'Isometric Overview'.

A Biological Science degree is desirable and also a working knowledge of Astrophysics and Biochemistry. 1000 + hours of in-house virtual experience and an ability to pass a physical examination to specific mission standards. [Hand + Eye Co-ordination.] Psychological evaluation is assessed from free-flowing interviews, observations and other psych tests, although reliability is not always accurate.

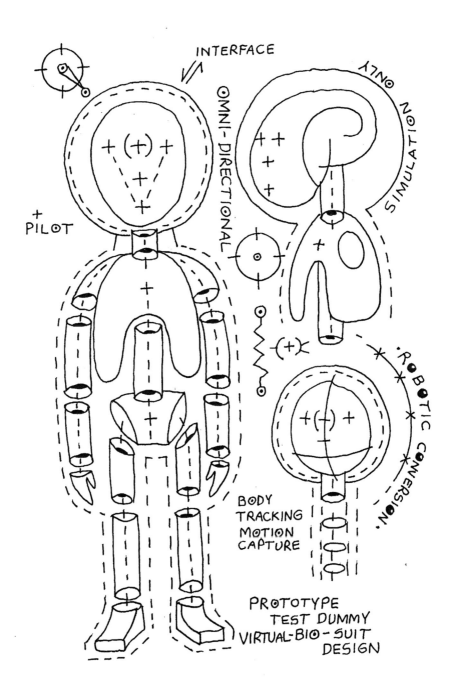

INTERFACE

OMNI-DIRECTIONAL

SIMULATION ONLY

PILOT

ROBOTIC CONVERSION

BODY
TRACKING
MOTION
CAPTURE

PROTOTYPE
TEST DUMMY
VIRTUAL-BIO-SUIT
DESIGN

65

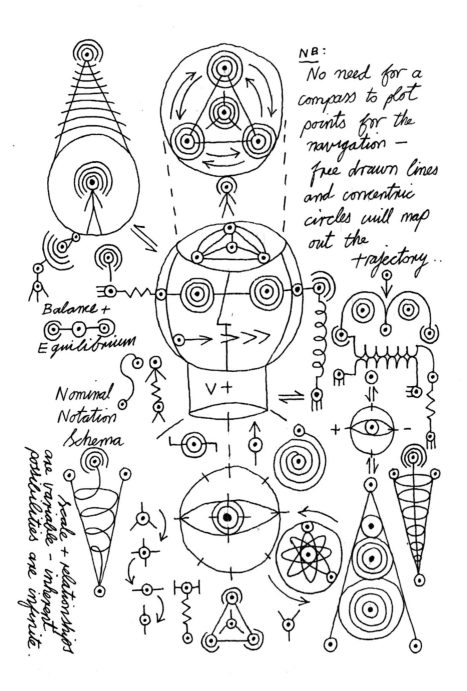

NB:
No need for a compass to plot points for the navigation — free drawn lines and concentric circles will map out the trajectory...

Balance + Equilibrium

Nominal Notation Schema

scale + relationships are variable — inherent possibilities are infinite.

V +

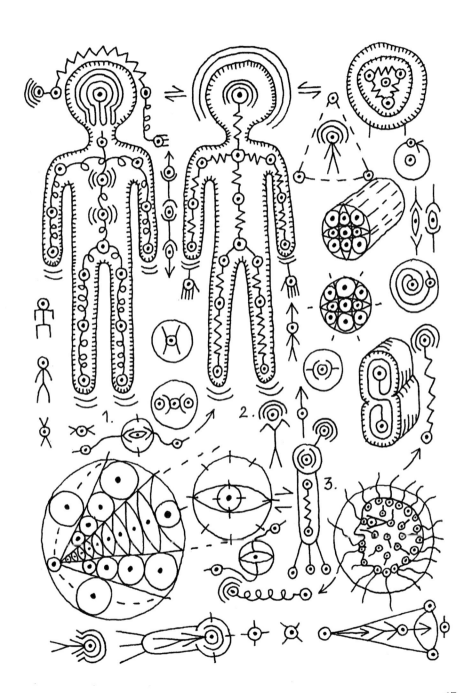

'Doug', he said, don't ever be a rocket
man.' I stopped. 'I mean it', he said.
'Because when you're out there you want
to be here, and when you're here you want
to be out there. Don't start that. Don't let
it get a hold of you.'

Ray Bradbury, 'Rocket Man'

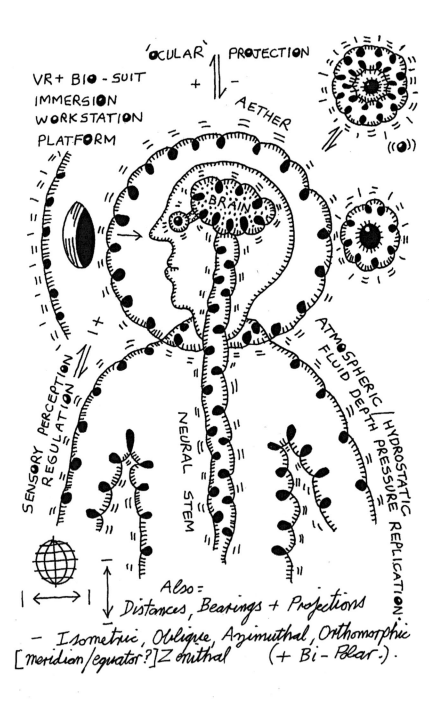

'OCULAR' PROJECTION

VR + BIO - SUIT
IMMERSION
WORKSTATION
PLATFORM

+ −

AETHER

((◉))

BRAIN

SENSORY PERCEPTION REGULATION

NEURAL STEM

ATMOSPHERIC / HYDROSTATIC FLUID DEPTH PRESSURE REPLICATION.

Also =
Distances, Bearings + Projections
— Isometric, Oblique, Azimuthal, Orthomorphic
[meridian/equator?] Zenithal   (+ Bi-Polar.)

High Definition, Stereoscopic 3D visor screen – eye to 'eye' bio-electrical feedback – multicellular input systems function. The feeling of being totally embedded and immersed in the world of the Ocularis environment.

Video scanning processors – 1000 + LUX.

'Reality' Visor:
- cognition
- adaptation
- communication
- efficiency
- connectivity

MAGNIFIED DETAIL

CONVERGENCE

PLASMA BULB OR CELL(S)

ATOMS | FREE
IONS | ELECTRONS

GLASS

BIOGLOVE HAND CONTROLS

consciousness
light perception
and vision + stability
Pixel orbiter

LOW LUMINANCE DARK-ROOM
colour BLACK LEVEL!

PLASMA MESH / MATRIX

·FLAT SCREEN

continuous mapping (grid)
- possibility of screen burn-out?
upgrade = OLED Organic Light Emitting Diode

NB:- Some image retention 'ghosting' in the optimised optical visor

Low Visibility
- motion blur
- lens - colour stability
+ total Human Eye-to-Brain receptivity.

71

High definition virtual images – present 'instant' with no delay. Possible hallucination of the endless and some degree of difficulty in locking onto a fixed point in space. Only the inertia of the 'real'.

Accelerated perspective
– possibly problematic
– inertia of the body
– lack of mass in the virtual environment
– lack of movement + physical displacement.

Disorientation – disorder of the senses caused by imagined weightlessness. 'stop in time' at the vanishing point of the virtual event horizon.

ULTRAFAST
VOYEUR / VOYAGER
Temporal Anomalies?

The plot in VR – The being of virtual trajectory free of all resistance – Freefall?

Isolation distorts perspective = Zone displacement

A loss of how to exist as a being in the 'real' world.

'LOSS OF EARTH' vertigo caused by depth of field within the 'spectacle'

Loss of movement in the body in the 'real' world
– a loss of 'Terra Firma'

+
V R

72

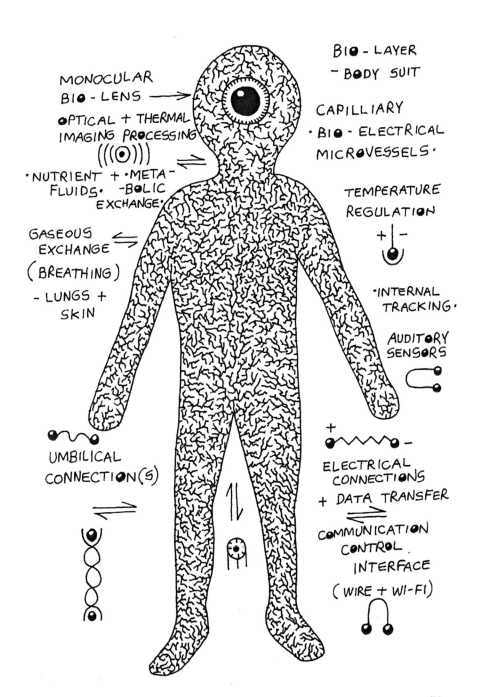

MONOCULAR
BIO-LENS →

OPTICAL + THERMAL
IMAGING PROCESSING
$(((\odot)))$ ⇌

·NUTRIENT + ·META-
FLUIDS· -BOLIC
EXCHANGE·

GASEOUS ⇐
EXCHANGE
(BREATHING)
- LUNGS + SKIN

UMBILICAL
CONNECTION(S)

⇒

BIO-LAYER
-BODY SUIT

CAPILLIARY
·BIO-ELECTRICAL
MICROVESSELS·

TEMPERATURE
REGULATION
+ | -

·INTERNAL
TRACKING·

AUDITORY
SENSORS

+
-
ELECTRICAL
CONNECTIONS
+ DATA TRANSFER
⇌
COMMUNICATION
CONTROL·
INTERFACE
(WIRE + WI-FI)

73

The Body Suit is formed from several layers – membranes comprising both electrical and bio-electrical elements. There is an external virtual input.

Around the body suit is the virtual isolation flotation pod – sound-proofed and a very low-light environment.

The saline solution keeps the suit at an even body temperature – additional thermal control is conducted via the suit itself.

The saline solution in the floatation pod gives the feeling of floating or weightlessness + is designed to give the feeling that is similar to being submersed / submerged in the fluid environment of Ocularis.

MONOCULAR · VISOR ·

TOTAL ISOLATION

EXPERIENCE OF WEIGHTLESSNESS

DIM BACKGROUND LIGHTING

SENSOR POINTS

NaCl-SALINE SOLUTION @ 41 30% – DENSITY ≅ 1·240 kg/L

NaCl + H_2O

UMBILICAL FEED
+ / –

DATA FEED
+ / –

Computer monitoring systems + feedback control.

A monocular Visor is fitted so as to closely reproduce the environ-mental conditions seen on Ocularis

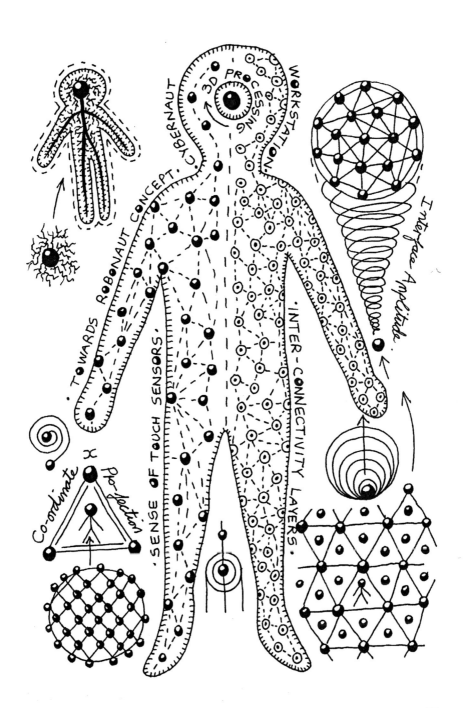

. TOWARDS ROBONAUT CONCEPT . CYBERNAUT

3D PROCESSING

WORKSTATION.

Interface Amplitude. ←

. INTER-CONNECTIVITY LAYERS.

. SENSE OF TOUCH SENSORS .

Co-ordinate x

Pro-jection

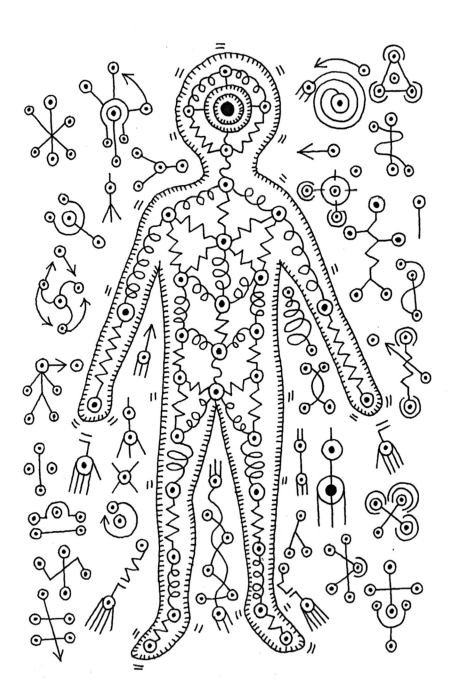

Key aspects of the mission should not be overlooked —
by the very nature of the exploration the cybernaut / virtual astronaut also becomes the very first aquanaut in the virtual field + and in virtual aquanautics. Studies of elements of marine science, the ecosystem, fluid dynamics, chemical fluxes, hydrography, hydrology, paleoceanography and internal tides + currents. The virtual cybernaut / aquanaut is an oceanic exploration platform in articulated anthropomorphic form.

Ocularis Blue/Green Spectrum + OCULARIS

Deep I. immersion ↓ pH ≈ 8·2

Cybernaut

Virtual Deep-Sea

Virtual buoyancy

Aquanaut

Navigation + burrow

NB: Focus, Precision (?) Planning + Discipline (+)

Virtual sub-marine platform

Diving Bio-suit

Virtual Astronaut — Clothed — micro fabric and Argon gas thermal layer

'Personal Climate': micro-rubberised Neoprene fabric...

The virtual bio-suit has all bio-exchange requirements optimised, although the layers or skins of the suit limit movement + dexterity somewhat — ergonomics of body movement are limited, but this is compensated for by the range of touch controls in the suit + bio-electric sensors.

77

Sense of touch added to previously only visual connectivity.
3D Visualisation - processing and analysis. Realistic computational interaction tools.
'Real World action - Isometrics.'
- User input + feedback.
Holographic Projection.

FEEDBACK
⇌
RESONANCE
'phantom pro-jection'
Haptic technology (sense of touch) 'HAPTICS'
Oscillating Electric Field →
+
Acoustic Radiation ultrasound

Accelerometers

Vibrotactile Effectors.

'Phantom Projection technology.
- Interact with physical objects in Virtual Reality through touch - interactivity in real-time with virtual objects...

magnetic field.

ENHANCED POWER.

Glove.

Tactile responses.

Shadow hand technology.

Pressure sensation hardware systems (+ other stimuli hardware)
Pressure sensation software system
Fluid interface vibration capabilities
- proximity sensors,
micro-gyroscopic facility
+
orientation sensors.

· TELEMATIC ·

HEAD VISOR
HAND To EYE +
TOUCH SCREEN /
CURSOR ANDROID.
OPERATING SYSTEM
- INTERFACE
TOUCH INPUTS

78

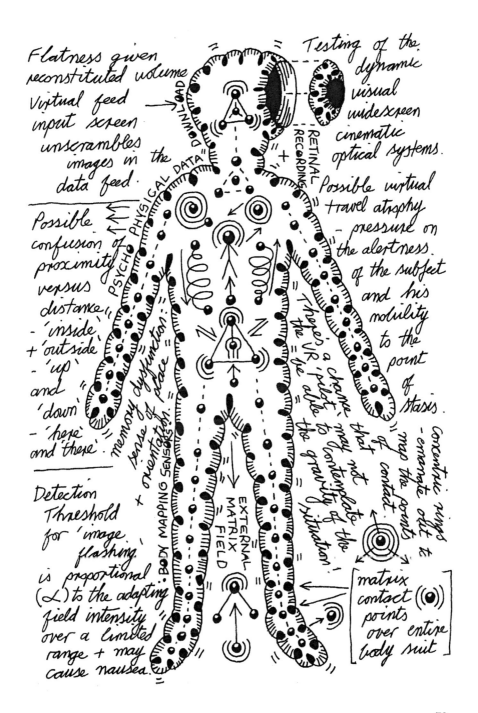

Flatness given reconstituted volume Virtual feed input screen unscrambles images in the data feed.

Testing of the dynamic visual widescreen cinematic optical systems.

"PHYSICAL DATA DOWNLOAD"

RETINAL RECORDING

Possible confusion of proximity versus distance. - 'inside' + 'outside' - 'up' and 'down' - 'here' and 'there'.

PSYCHO PHYSICAL DATA

memory dysfunction: sense of place + orientation: BODY MAPPING SENSORS.

Possible virtual travel atrophy - pressure on the alertness of the subject and his mobility to the point of stasis.

There's a chance that the VR 'pilot' may not be able to contemplate the gravity of the situation!

Concentric rings - emanate out & map the points of contact.

Detection Threshold for 'image flashing' is proportional ($\propto$) to the adapting field intensity over a limited range + may cause nausea.

EXTERNAL MATRIX FIELD

[matrix contact points over entire body suit]

Briefly, the pros + cons of virtual planetary exploration are as follows:
Psychological effects — short-term intensified isolation, claustrophobia limited physical mobility fatigue, possible anxiety, some possible subsequent post-exploration insomnia, falling levels of concentration.

This may lead to psychiatric disorders and lower personal performance — psychosis — (paranoid delusions)!

Altered states and sensory overload may also result from prolonged immersion in the floatation pod and virtual reality body suit re-adjustment could be problematic.

The Brain can also mis-identify the source of what is being experienced ...

... Faulty Source Monitoring + Memory Reflux. It is no coincidence that the mission control has come to name the pod & the body suit as 'the Sarcophagus.'

NO COSMIC RADIATION

NO BLOOD CELL OR BONE CHANGE

MUSCLE LOSS

NO DETRIMENTAL EFFECTS OF NO GRAVITY

NO 'BIO-ELECTRICAL FEEDBACK LAYER'

THERMAL CONTROL LAYER

INPUT + OUTPUT

NO SPACE SICKNESS

NO DAMAGED IMMUNE SYSTEM

NO CIRCULATORY PROBLEMS

The exploration to connect the imagined environment and so-called 'primitive' nature of Ocularis with the digital 'space age' technology of the Human World of Earth - a connection between planets in a search for the essence of everything.

The eventual ability to scrutinize every square centimetre of the planet via virtual projection - an expansion of the world of human experience + vision - albeit in a slightly fragmented version

[The materiality (and the immateriality) transmitted from wires and cables and on into cyberspace / hyperspace aether.]

of reality (where perception becomes a process) - transcending spatial limitations - the nature of 'reality' becomes fluid - expansion of the present into the future and the stimulation of all the senses and on into mind altering experiences . . . .

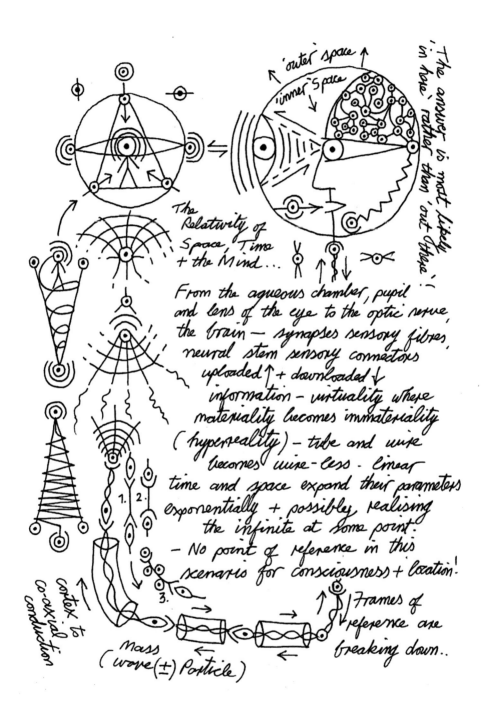

'outer space'

'inner space'

The answer is most likely 'in here' rather than 'out there'!

The Relativity of Space, Time + the Mind...

From the aqueous chamber, pupil and lens of the eye to the optic nerve, the brain — synapses sensory fibres, neural stem sensory connectors uploaded↑ + downloaded↓ information — virtuality where materiality becomes immateriality (hyperreality) — tube and wire becomes wire-less. Linear time and space expand their parameters exponentially + possibly realising the infinite at some point. — No point of reference in this scenario for consciousness + location! Frames of reference are breaking down..

1. 2.

3.

cortex to co-axial conduction

Mass (wave(±) Particle)

The artists of the new century wanted to penetrate deeper, to show things as they were under the surface, or as they might have been had the visible and tangible world always corresponded with the intangible and the spiritual. They wanted to extend the domain of art beyond the boundaries of the actual, so as to include the imagined, the dreamt and the foreseen. They wanted more than anything else to express themselves.

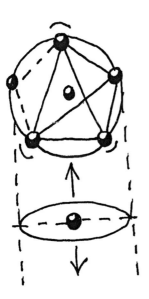

Edith Hoffmann, 'Expressionism: Movements in Modern Art' series [1956]

Initial studies have shown changes in psychological, psychosocial, cognitive and physiological effects — Humans are neurophysiologically wired to interpret stimuli and so there is the very real danger that the immersed cybernaut may not be able to re-engage with the 'real' world.

The Human brain may be unable to process the leap into the virtual reality projected 'alien' experience of Ocularis. Studies are at an early stage and only time will tell....

84

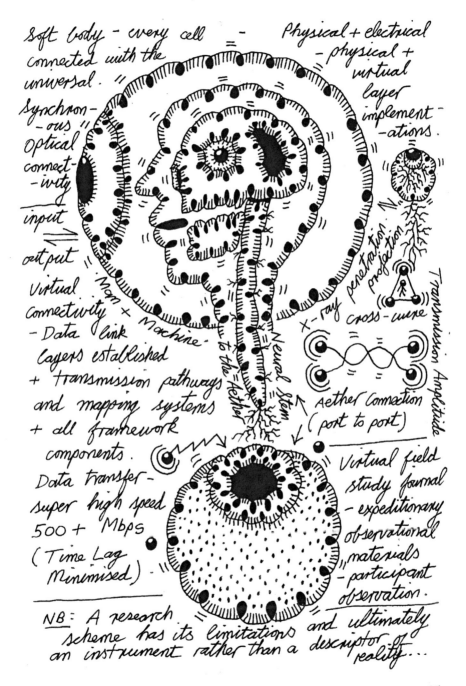

soft body – every cell connected with the universal.

Synchron--ous Optical connect--ivity

input

output

Virtual connectivity + – Data link Layers established + transmission pathways and mapping systems + all framework components. Data transfer- super high speed 500+ Mbps (Time Lag Minimised)

Man + Machine

to the Aether

Neural Stem

Physical + electrical – physical + virtual layer implement--ations.

X-ray penetration projection

cross-wire

Aether Connection (port to port)

Transmission Amplitude

Virtual field study journal – expeditionary observational materials – participant observation.

NB: A research scheme has its limitations and ultimately an instrument rather than a descriptor of reality...

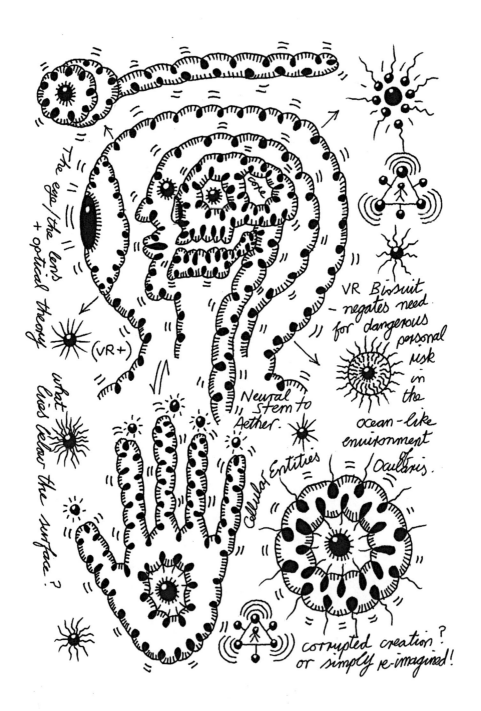

The eye / the lens / + optical theory

core

(VR+)

what lies below the surface?

Neural Stem to Aether.

Cellular Entities

VR Bissuit – negates need for dangerous personal risk in the ocean-like environment of Ocularis.

corrupted creation? or simply re-imagined!

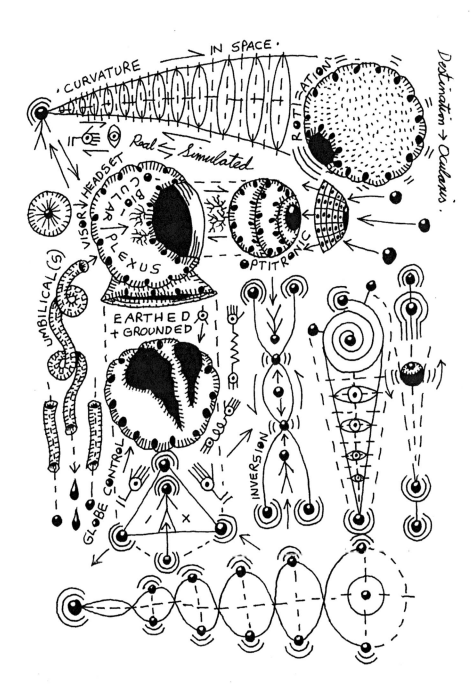

87

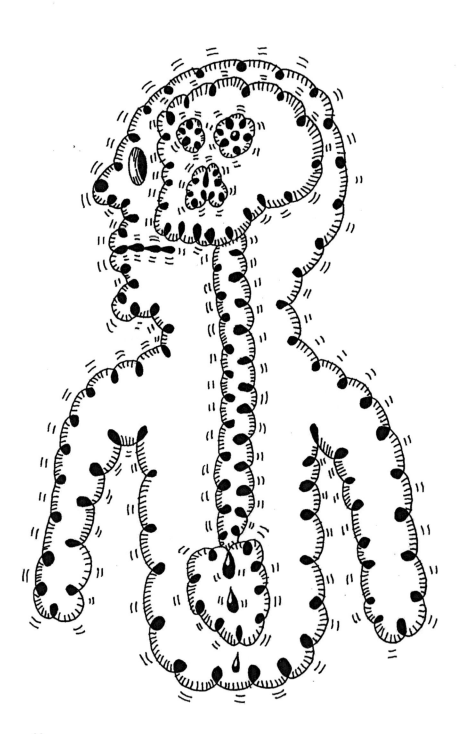

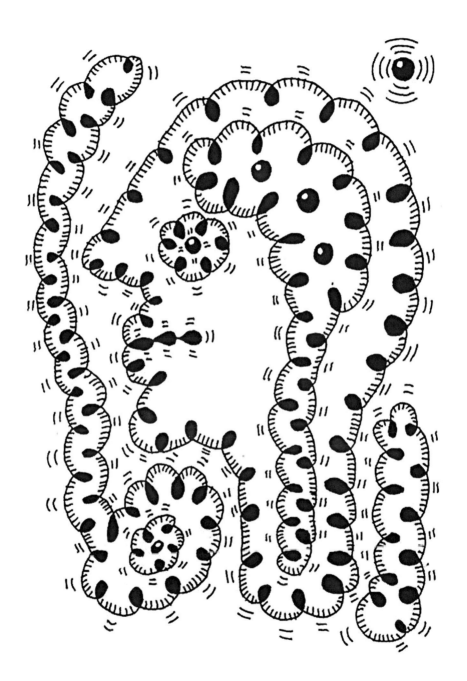

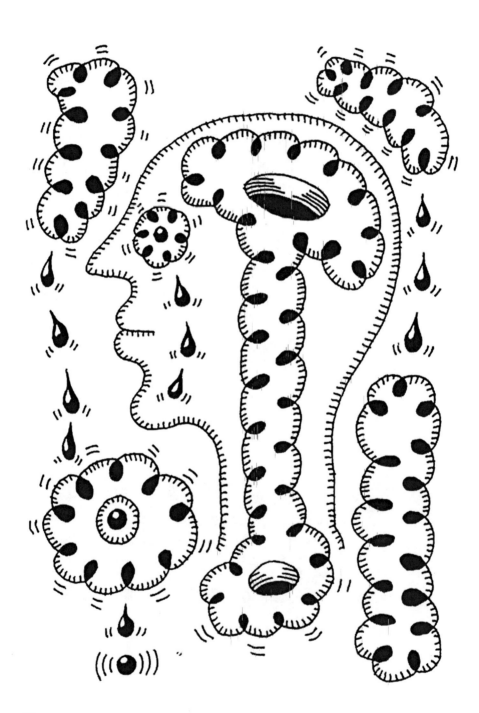

Space flights are merely an escape, a fleeing away from oneself, because it is easier to go to Mars or to the moon than it is to penetrate one's own being.

Carl Jung

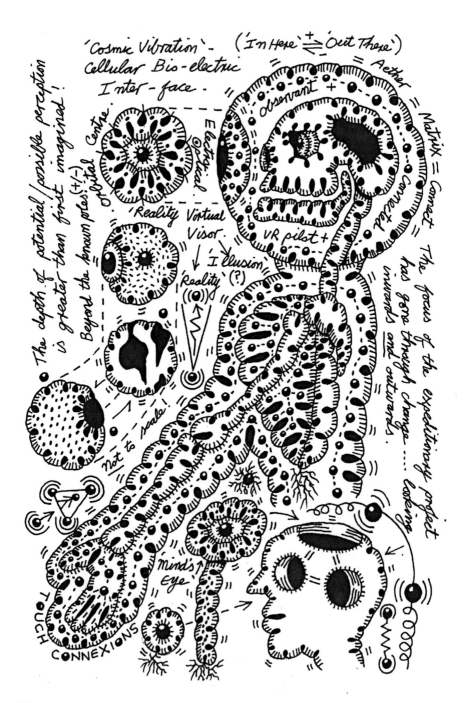

'Cosmic Vibration' - ('In Here ⇌ Out There')
Cellular Bio-electric
    Inter-face.

= Aether = Matrix = Connect = The focus of the expeditionary project has gone through change ..... looking inwards and outwards.

Observant +

Electrical Orbital Centre.

'Reality Virtual Visor.

↓ 'Illusion' (?)

'Reality.
((◉))

VR pilot +

Connected

The depth of potential/possible perception is greater than first imagined!
Beyond the known pres.(+/-)

Orbital Centre.

Not to scale!

Mind's Eye

TOUCH CONNEXIONS

The Mind's Eye is exploding: The Mind's Eye Gone Blind.

The visual cortex is disrupted. + all cognitive processing has stalled. All external and internal data is occluded. Sensory Overload— Thinking is most definitely very confused and distracted.

Head Space— Frustration, Helplessness, Hopelessness Hallucination (N,N-Dimethyltryptamine) Misinterpretation, Depression claustrophobia Too Much+ Pressure— Total Mental Dis- -Integration - out of control and staring into the Void....

In the realm of precision, planning, discipline and control, the ethereal mesh of the cosmos is disintegrating! Psychonaut Psychosis

cybernaut
Virtual Astronaut
Virtual Journey

Fatigue and lack of function leads me to believe that this may possibly be a mission fail(ure).

93

Exploration can express a genuine wish to innovate, to find new ideas, new means of expression. It can also express a refusal to face the realities of an existing situation. What the explorer brings back with him will after all be measured in terms of that situation. It is of little use to bring back home the future if it is only used as wallpaper for covering the cracks of the present.

David Downing, 'Future Rock'

This is the fragmented and somewhat incomplete annotated and abridged observer's log-book entries (subject to rigorous edited revisions, self censorship and subsequent omissions) for the first (and possibly only) explorative mission to the Planet Ocularis.

Most is 'fact', although some elements of hallucination, dream and visual distortion have potentially filtered into the narrative, descriptions and attempted visual notation and documentation.

Sometimes it has become difficult to separate 'visions' of 'reality' from those of deceptive illusion and confusion.

The trauma of virtual reality cyberspace wormhole projection has proved problematic in presenting a coherent and complete overview of the project.

The eye and the brain are seemingly deceived on many occasions within the context of the virtual environment, particularly when applied to this projection into a distant alien world such as Ocularis.

Errors are always likely to occur during virtual reality cyberspace wormhole connections.

Travelling at the speed of thought (or maybe light) –
Passing through the synapses of the Brain, through
convoluted passages and pathways and on into the
darkest regions of deep, real and imagined space(s).
Travelling in the vast ocean of the Id ..... and beyond.

To go where no explorer has been before – through
observations, notions, ideas and thought processes.

From the Aether and from the neural stem – the Brain,
the Mind, the conscious and the subconscious,
Frontal lobes – Cerebellum, Cerebrum, Medullary
Cortex – Tracing a journey through Space and
Time ..... or wherever (or whatever).

Disembodied thoughts becoming embedded in the
brain. Absorbing images and sensations quite unlike
anything ever seen before – ensuing hallucinations
and chronic mis-readings of information are therefore
inevitable.

Lately my fear has been creeping in to my feelings — if I stopped here for too long, I would cease to be human and I'd either have to face the reality of the situation or fall into the abyss .... I have to write, just in case I lose my mind and lose time and space in this isolated place .... and yet, I am compelled to do this.

I will write everything down and try to document it as best I can ..... time and space drift away from me constantly and only my visual display data gives me any indication as to my present situation.

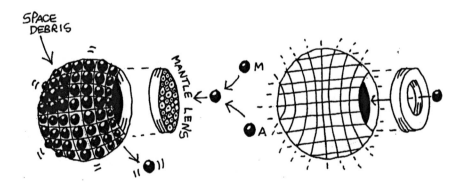

SPACE
DEBRIS

MANTLE LENS

M

A

Somebody help me, I'm missing,
somebody help me, I'm missing now
Touch with my mind, I have no frame,
touch with my mind, I have no frame
Well, now where is the time and who
the hell am I
Here floating in an aimless way?
No one knows where we are, they can't
feel us precisely
There is no fear here, how could such a
thing exist in this place
Where living and knowing and being
have never been heard of?
Have never been heard of?
Doomed to vanish in the flickering
light, disappearing to a darker night
Doomed to wander in a living death,
living anti-matter, anti-breath
Somebody help me, I'm losing,
somebody help me, I'm losing now
People around, there's no one to touch,
people around, no one to touch
I am now, quite alone, part of a vacant
time zone, floating in the void
Only dimly aware of existence, a dimly,
existing awareness
I am the lost one, I am the one you
fear, I am the lost one
I am the one who pressed through
space or stayed where I was
Or didn't exist in the first place.

Van der Graaf Generator, 'Pioneers Over C'

My psychological problems seem to be increasing. Trauma, space psychosis, virtual shock and sensory overload feed my waking thoughts and even my dreams.

Lately, fear and dread have been creeping into my observations and reports ..... if I remain in here for too long, I could / would cease to be human.

I have to document as accurately as I can, just in case I lose my mind.

Time and Space drift away from me constantly and only my sensory data displays give me any indication as to my exact situation.

Emergency extraction from the mainframe is imminent — input and feedback circuits are overloaded and my brain is fried ......

Cyber connections are corrupted ....
    Break the transmission feed
      Terminate now!
        mission message ends.......

The incomplete log entry page extracts were
obtained from an unknown/unidentified/un-named and
unverifiable source.

Some, but not all of the hand-written notation
and accompanying drawings/diagrams appear to
come from a pre/post exploration phase, although
some printout material from electronic note-pad
observations would also seem to be included here.

The current whereabouts and mental/physical state
of the author of these log book pages is unknown
and no statement from any official source is
available at this current time.

Author Unknown

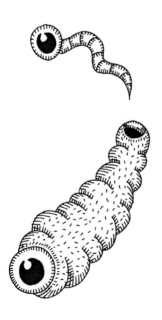

The creation of Ocularis - Water - cosmic dust and debris - light - life = protoplasm - cells - protozoa - flagellates - ciliates - amoeboids - soft-bodied invertebrates and the evolution of the life-force of Ocularis itself.

A _hypothesis_ for the formation of the planet = Formed from water vapour and gases - the initial hot atmosphere collected these elements together with dust and space debris - the water vapour condensed into an unbroken blanket of cloud through which the light from distant suns + stars could not penetrate the gloomy depths beneath.

Rain fell unceasingly from the upper strata of the 'world-cloud' atmosphere — steam gradually turned into water and concentrated.

An initial mantle-crust formed and the ocean developed from the violent rain storms.

The cloud blanket eventually thinned —growing thinner and thinner, breaking apart and for the first time rays of cosmic light could shine into the darkness of the waters on/in Ocularis —

— Light in the blue-green spectrum which becomes dimmer and darker until there is still just blackness in the depths of Ocularis.

The early days of Ocularis were those of a lifeless sphere-oid. It is not known how the spark of life first flickered into being on the planet, but the first living things were most likely specks and spots of protoplasmic material — — neither 'plant' nor 'animal' — clear jelly-like globules of microscopic protoplasm and then ovaloid single-cells which eventually congregated, communed, coalesced and conjoined.

The first proper cells were probably free-floating microscopic bodies with a nucleus and other particles within a gel membrane. The very first life was probably simpler than cells, but somehow cells spontaneously developed and evolved into single cell organisms. These earliest cells will have contained all the possibilities for the evolution of life on Ocularis.

Life began in this ocean — living, fluid organisms drifting and swimming in the dim light and darkness.

Lifeless matter spontaneously evolved into unknown biological living material and began its range of evolutionary processes — perhaps in this part of the universe there is a universal scientific principle that life and evolution operate as automatically as that of gravitational pull.

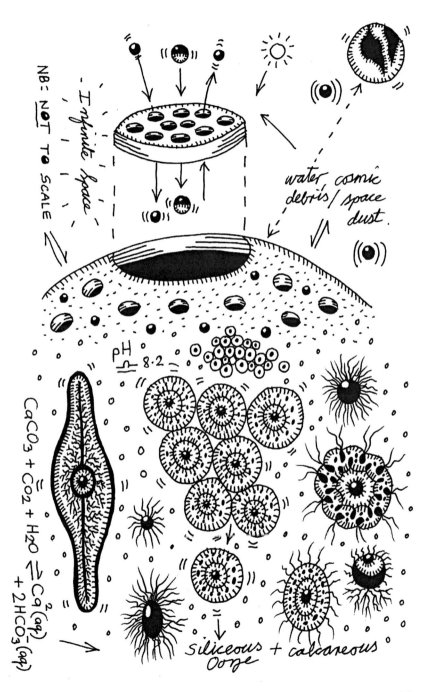

NB: NOT TO SCALE

- Infinite space -

water, cosmic debris / space dust.

pH 8.2

$$CaCO_3 + CO_2 + H_2O \rightleftharpoons Ca^{2+}(aq) + 2HCO_3^-(aq)$$

siliceous + calcareous
Ooze

The ability of Ocularis to focus its gaze on a distant planet Earth and to mimetically + spontaneously create organisms, albeit in a distorted and incomplete form.

Often the microscopic becomes the macroscopic (and vice versa).

Certain types of organisms seem to have been selected and reproduced in preference to others. Predominantly those of an aquatic nature (so obvious considering the fluid environment of Ocularis). Mostly soft-bodied invertebrates, and almost no emphasis on the replication of 'hard bone' vertebrate forms although some duplication of vaguely 'human' characteristics (particularly the brains, eyes and nervous systems) in some of these soft-bodied organisms seems to be taking shape – some kind of conscious selection is in operation.

A veritable organic laboratory – spontaneously self-creating and evolving in deep space. Almost like the distorted and eccentric thoughts of the planet itself.

Creatures of the psychic abyss – the streams of consciousness arising from the darkest recesses of the primitive mind.

Primordial darkness and chaos – refining and evolving over vast periods of time.

In parts, proto-humanoid. Proto-embryonic development......the creatures may even eventually develop back-bones........

organic / inorganic – invertebrates become vertebrates – complex organisms, bacilli, bacteria, viruses and on into single cell and multi cellular organisms – symbiotic and mutualist in communities and societies of cells and organisms.

Soft bodies in an ocean of fluid flow – a contained universe of mutating change. From the primal ooze of star-seeded dust – organisms spontaneously came into life and evolved and developed over millenia – a mere blink of the eye in the 'mind' of the universe.

The evolution - periodic proto-plasmic evocations + archaeological psycho - fossilisation.

The ocular orbits and the development of the senses. The complexities of creation and the spontaneous processes of growth and of development.

Their scope is the realm of potential and of fantastic possibilities ....

Microbes to molluscs, single cells to the complexities of cell communities, neural networks and inter-connections of organisms swimming in the Ocularis ocean gene pool - micro becomes macro in the spontaneous streams of oceanic consciousness.

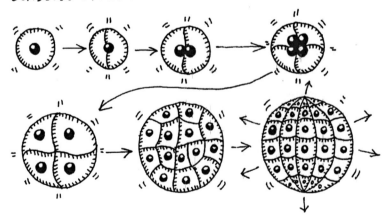

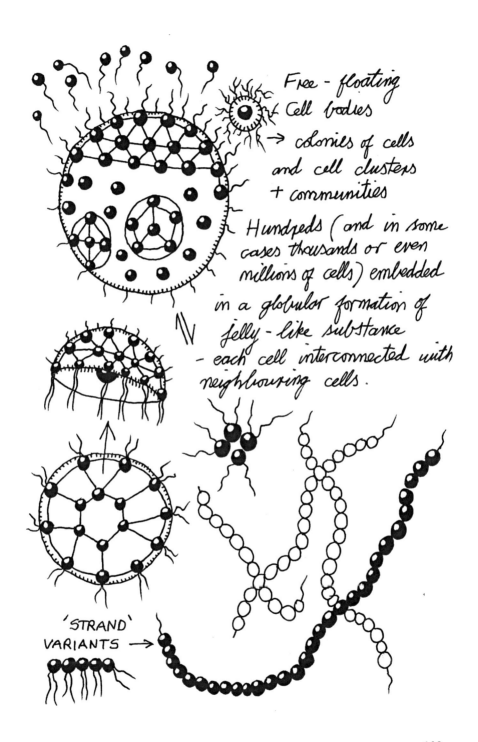

Free - floating
Cell bodies
→ colonies of cells
and cell clusters
+ communities

Hundreds (and in some
cases thousands or even
millions of cells) embedded
in a globular formation of
jelly - like substance
- each cell interconnected with
neighbouring cells.

'STRAND'
VARIANTS →

109

A 'watery world' — a slow formation + an aggregation of cells into social structures — communicating entities. Some elements of calcified fragments utilised to form living beings that both respond to and emit light. An 'ocean' of floaters carried on the convection currents.

More complex living structures have evolved — some living deep down in the dark ooze layer — laid down over millions of years.

Minerals + salts bubbling up through the aqueous miasma

The microscopic becomes the macroscopic (and vice versa).

A veritable organic laboratory spontaneously self-created and evolved in the deepest, darkest recesses of the known universe. At times, it seems as though these interconnected creatures are almost the distorted and eccentric thoughts of the planet itself ....

Amoeboid - Micro to Macro - some large enough to project / dive into the interstitial spaces within the gelatinous material.

Amoebae Protist - social + interactive.

Pseudopods / pseudopodia

Vacuoles - empty voids and also waste material

Water vacuoles - - H_2O and salts / minerals - Osmotic control.

Cell Membrane

Agglutinations of found materials - grains of Calcium and Silica + digested diatoms. - internal gelatinous fluids. Particles of detritus ingested by phagocytosis - Ectoplasmic. Endoplasm. Some of these large Amoeboids form larger organisms and structures.

Ocular Orbit - photosensitive / photoreceptive. - Energy absorption.

Nucleus - cell control + integrity

Cilia - - Filamentous extensions - Some variants of the Amoeboids exhibit extensions that aid movement and also attract detritus.

111

PHOTOLIPIDS

AMOEBOID

cohesive bonding

water (+VE) POLE
+
─ (─VE)
HYDROPHOBIC POLE

ABSORPTION OF FREE-FLOATING LIPID MOLECULES AND LARGE GLOBULES

[CELL WEIRD-NESS]

structural component in the cell membranes

- biochemical 'building blocks'
- biosynthetic pathways + cell functions.
- Lipid globules are bipolar - the positive pole aligns with the aqueous environment whilst the hydrophobic pole repels.

- Able to form membranes in the aqueous environment of Ocularis.
+
- Cell signalling receptors.

{ metabolite, } : metabolism + neural
{ metabolism } : activity + photosynthetic activity
O=P-OH : more biophysical research needed
[BIOSYNTHESIS.] PSYCHOPLASMOSIS.

112

Simple Gill Mechanism

'Eye-Pod Variants

Free-Swimming in a/the Cosmic Oceans

Rising from the Siliceous / Calcareous Ooze → Darkness into Light

113

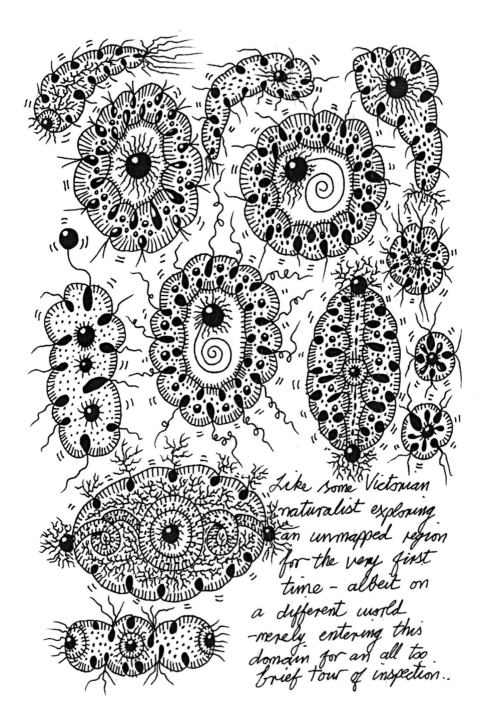

Like some Victorian naturalist exploring an unmapped region for the very first time - albeit on a different world - merely entering this domain for an all too brief tour of inspection..

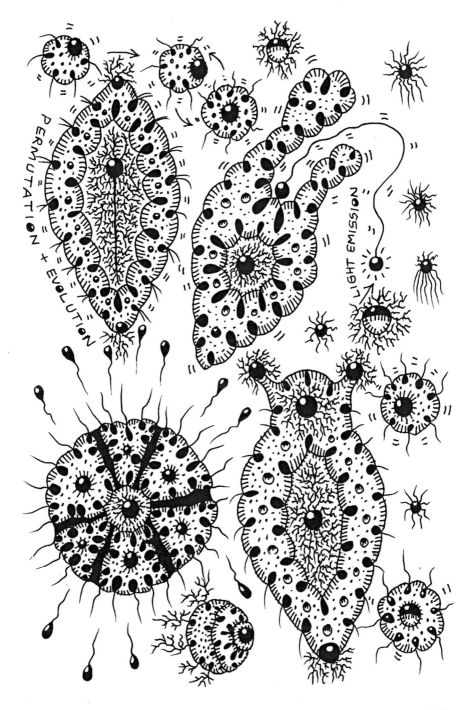

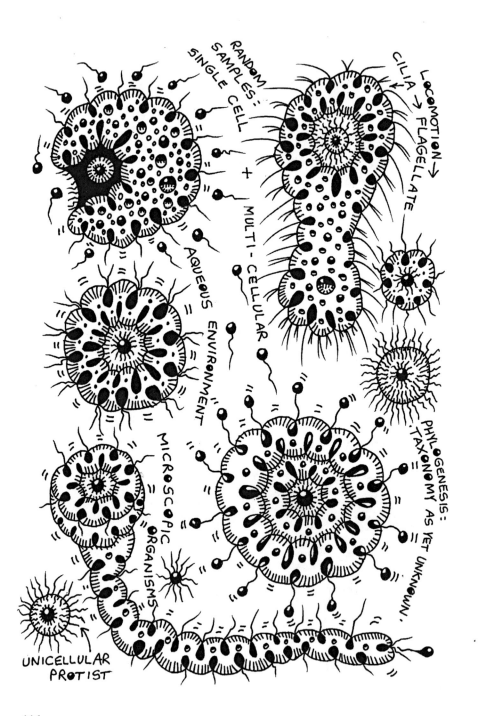

RANDOM
SAMPLES:
SINGLE CELL

+

MULTI-CELLULAR

LOCOMOTION:
CILIA → FLAGELLATE

AQUEOUS ENVIRONMENT

MICROSCOPIC ORGANISMS

PHYLOGENESIS: TAXONOMY AS YET UNKNOWN.

UNICELLULAR PROTIST

116

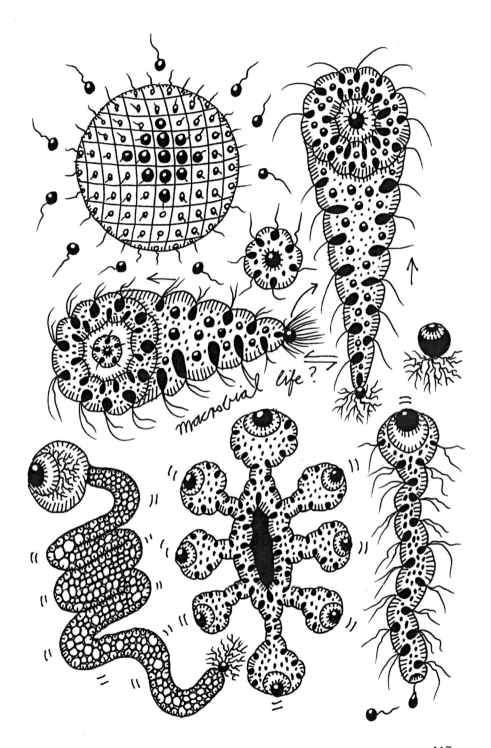

macrobial life?

117

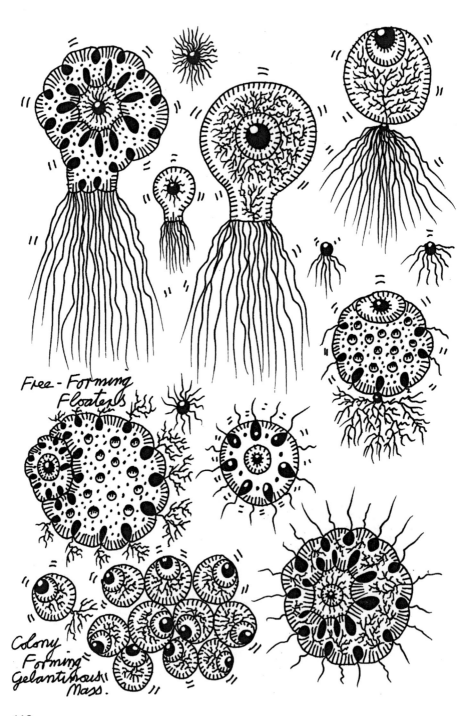

Free - Forming
Floaters

Colony
Forming
Gelantinous
Mass.

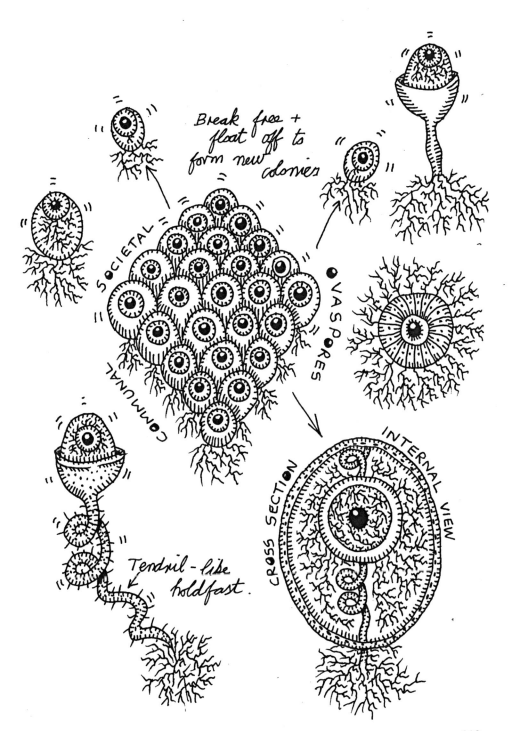

Break free + float off to form new colonies

SOCIETAL

COMMUNAL

OVASPORES

Tendril-like holdfast.

CROSS SECTION

INTERNAL VIEW

Electrically charged + bis-luminescent
Mutualist / symbiotic. photo-receptive.
From single,
primordial 'floaters'
to slow formations
of aggregations
of cells into social
structures and
interconnected
+ complex Zoomorphic
organisms. "

Free-floating
ambulatory,
swimming.

Both physical
 (touch)
and psychic links.

Spontaneous development
+ evolution – (rapid
evolutionary morphology).

– Mimetic memory - brains (branes?) + embryonic
humanoid - like, soft-bodied invertebrates.

"SWIMMING"
IN A
STREAM
OF
CONSCIOUSNESS.

PALEOZOID?

Zoomorphic

METAZOID?

'EYE-
-ATOMS
+
PROTO-
-SPORES.

·PSYCHO
PLANKTON

[HOLOZOIC
- INGESTION·
DIGESTION·
ABSORPTION·
·ASSIMILATION·EGESTION]

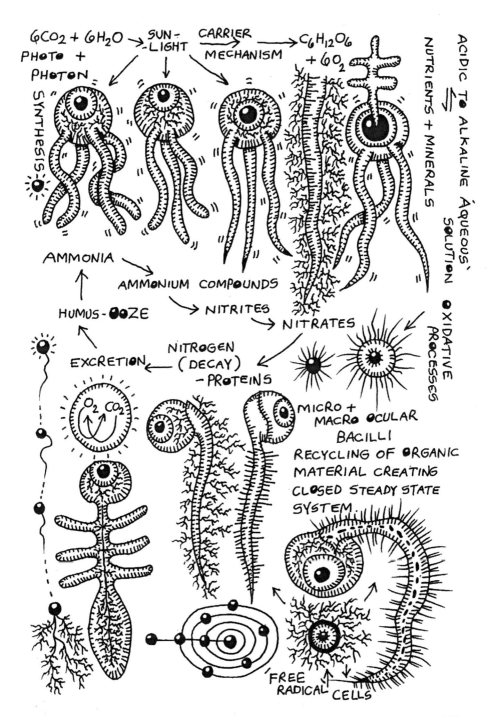

$6CO_2 + 6H_2O \rightarrow$ SUN-LIGHT $\rightarrow$ CARRIER MECHANISM $\rightarrow C_6H_{12}O_6 + 6O_2$

PHOTO + PHOTON

SYNTHESIS

ACIDIC TO ALKALINE AQUEOUS SOLUTION

NUTRIENTS + MINERALS

AMMONIA

AMMONIUM COMPOUNDS

HUMUS-OOZE

NITRITES

NITRATES

OXIDATIVE PROCESSES

EXCRETION

NITROGEN (DECAY) - PROTEINS

O_2 CO_2

MICRO + MACRO OCULAR BACILLI RECYCLING OF ORGANIC MATERIAL CREATING CLOSED STEADY STATE SYSTEM

FREE RADICAL CELLS

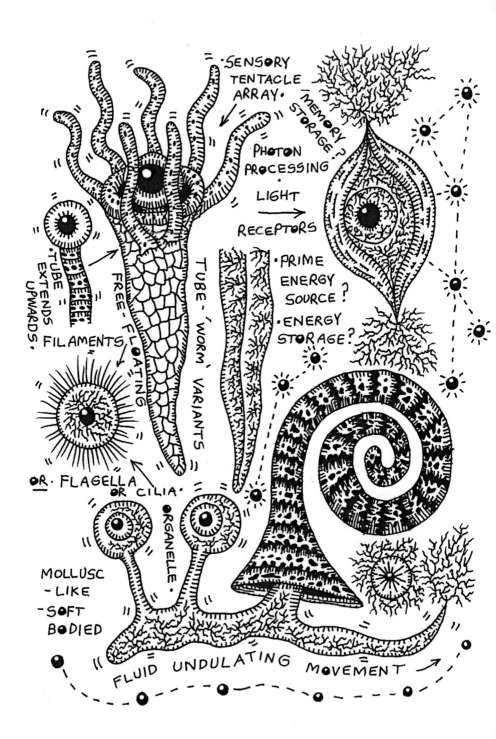

- SENSORY TENTACLE ARRAY -

MEMORY STORAGE ?

PHOTON PROCESSING

LIGHT →

RECEPTORS

- TUBE EXTENDS UPWARDS -

FREE-FLOATING

TUBE - 'WORM' VARIANTS

- PRIME ENERGY SOURCE ?
- ENERGY STORAGE ?

FILAMENTS

OR - FLAGELLA OR CILIA -

ORGANELLE -

MOLLUSC -LIKE -SOFT BODIED

FLUID UNDULATING MOVEMENT →

122

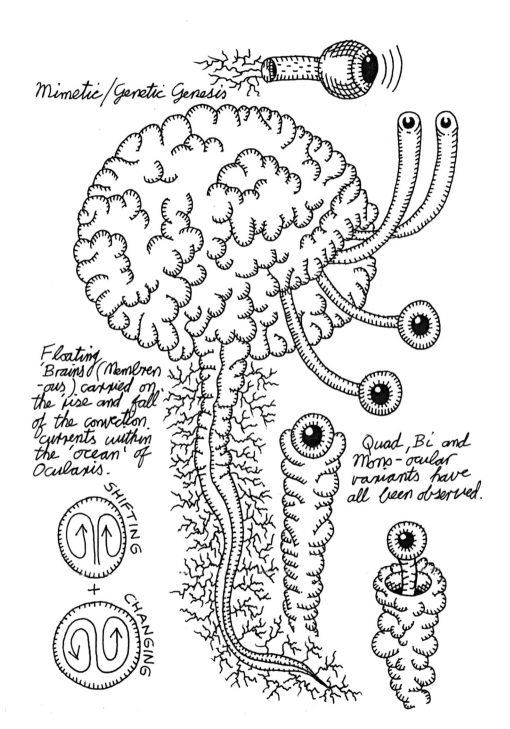

Mimetic/Genetic Genesis

Floating 'Brains' (Membren -ous) carried on the 'rise and fall of the convection currents within the 'ocean' of Ocularis.

SHIFTING

+

CHANGING

Quad, Bi and Mono-ocular variants have all been observed.

123

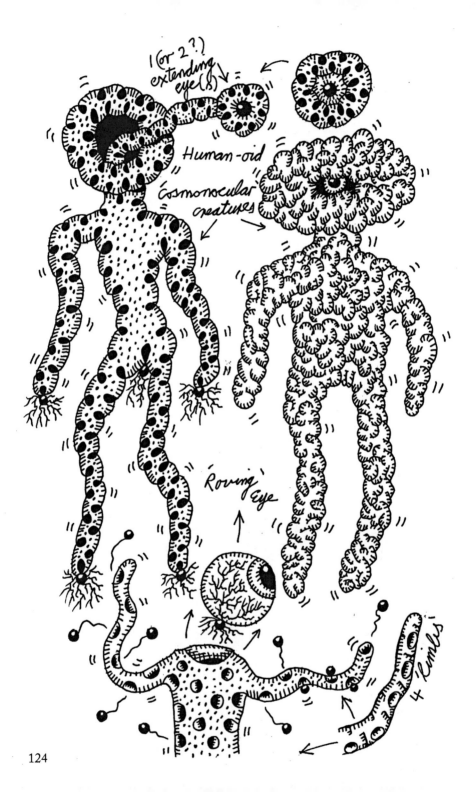

1 (or 2 ?)
extending
eye(s)

Human-oid
Cosmonocular
creatures

'Roving'
Eye

+ 'Rimles'

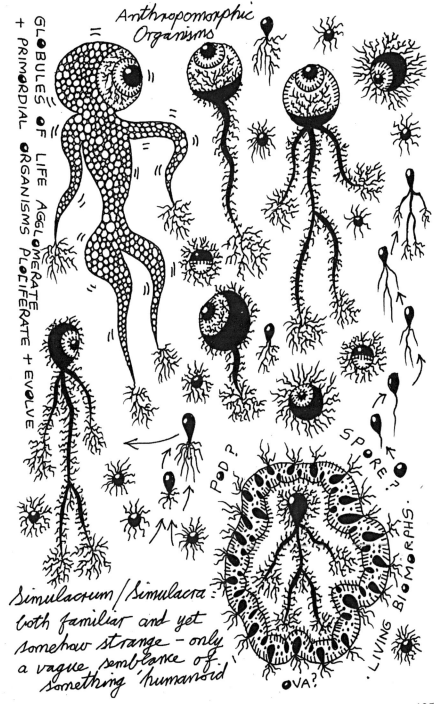

Anthropomorphic Organisms

GLOBULES OF LIFE AGGLOMERATE + PRIMORDIAL ORGANISMS PROLIFERATE + EVOLVE

POD ?.

SPORE ?.

LIVING BIOMORPHS.

OVA ?

Simulacrum / Simulacra: both familiar and yet somehow strange — only a vague semblance of something 'humanoid'

125

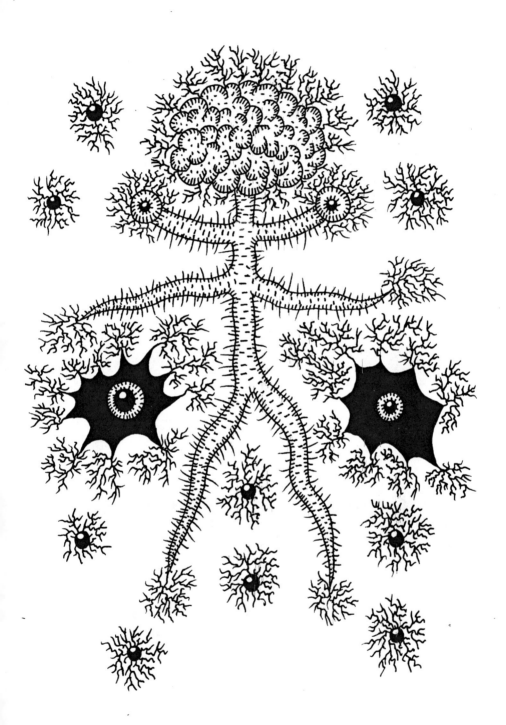

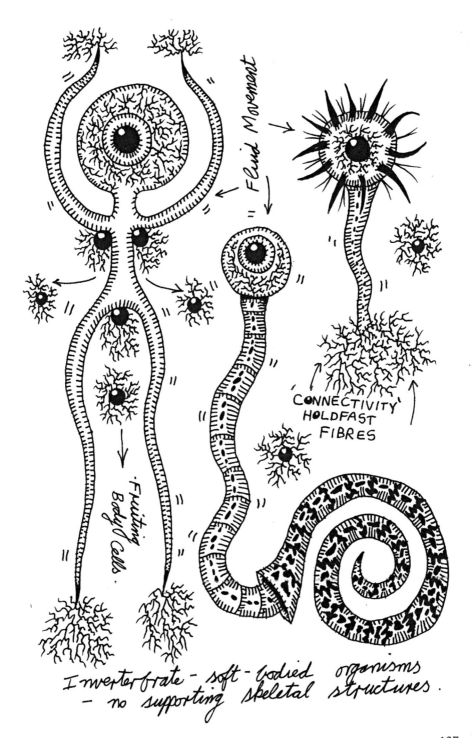

Fluid Movement

Fruiting Body Cells.

'CONNECTIVITY' HOLDFAST FIBRES

Invertebrate - soft - bodied organisms
- no supporting skeletal structures.

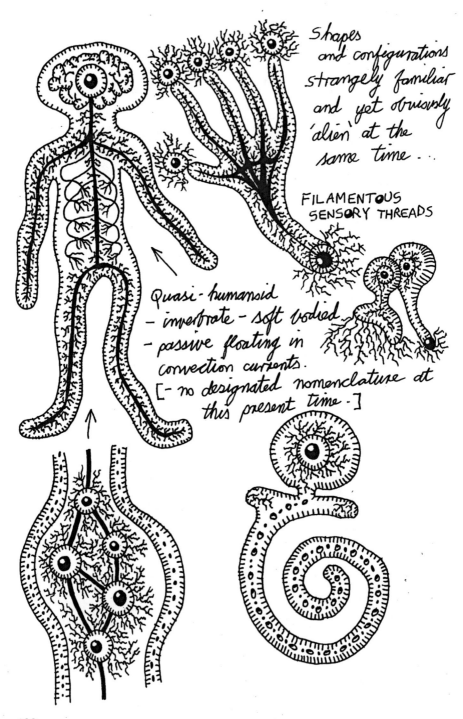

Shapes
and configurations
strangely familiar
and yet obviously
'alien' at the
same time...

FILAMENTOUS
SENSORY THREADS

Quasi-humanoid
– invertrate – soft bodied
– passive floating in
convection currents.
[– no designated nomenclature at
this present time.]

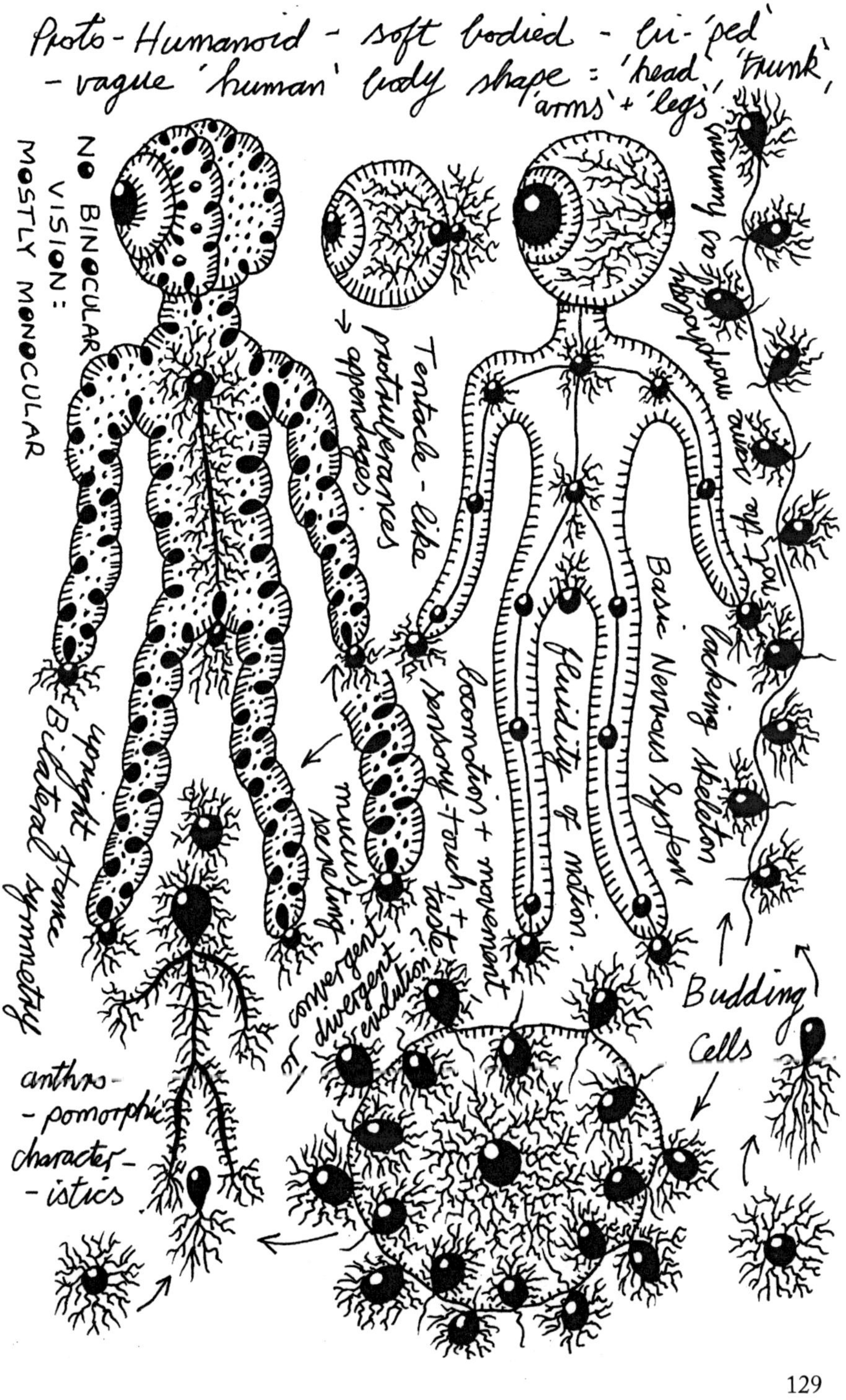

Proto-Humanoid - soft bodied - bi-'ped' - vague 'human' body shape = 'head', 'trunk', 'arms' + 'legs'

NO BINOCULAR VISION : MOSTLY MONOCULAR

Tentacle-like protuberances → appendages.

anomalous nervous system → branching skeleton

Basic Nervous System

fluidity of motion.

locomotion + movement

sensory - touch + taste - mucusting - secreting

of convergent or divergent evolution?

upright stance Bilateral symmetry

anthro- -pomorphic character- -istics

Budding Cells

129

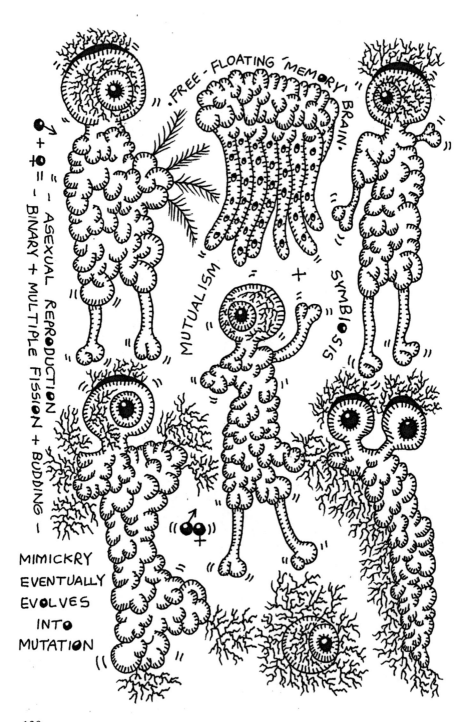

.FREE - FLOATING 'MEMORY' BRAIN.

♂ ⟋
+ =
♀ =
— ASEXUAL REPRODUCTION
— BINARY + MULTIPLE FISSION + BUDDING —

MUTUALISM

+

SYMBIOSIS

♂♀

MIMICKRY
EVENTUALLY
EVOLVES
INTO
MUTATION

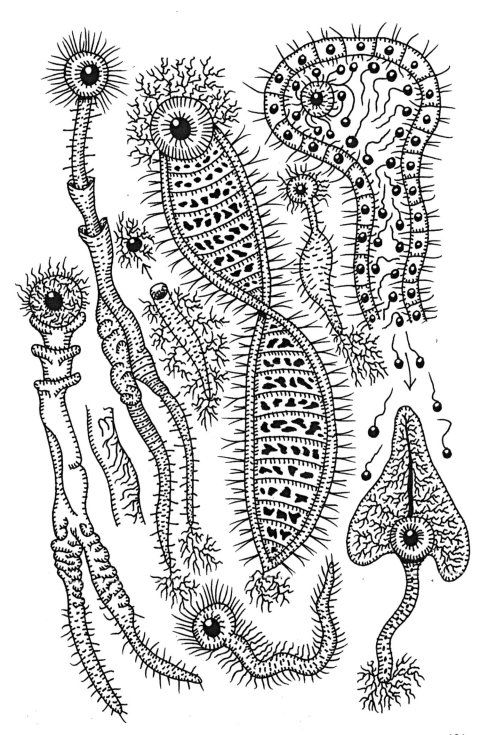

131

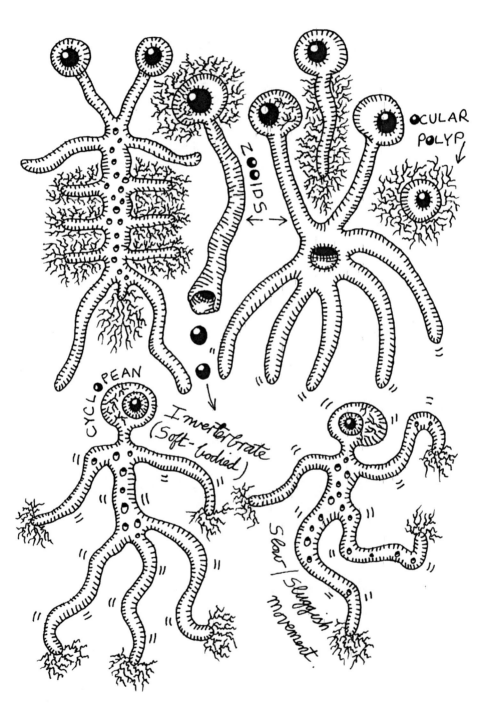

ZOOIDS

OCULAR POLYP

CYCLOPEAN

Invertebrate (Soft-bodied)

Slow/Sluggish movement.

132

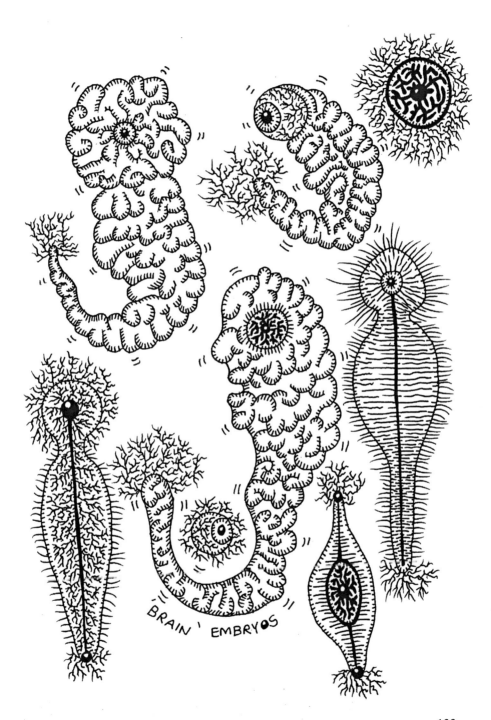

"BRAIN" EMBRYOS

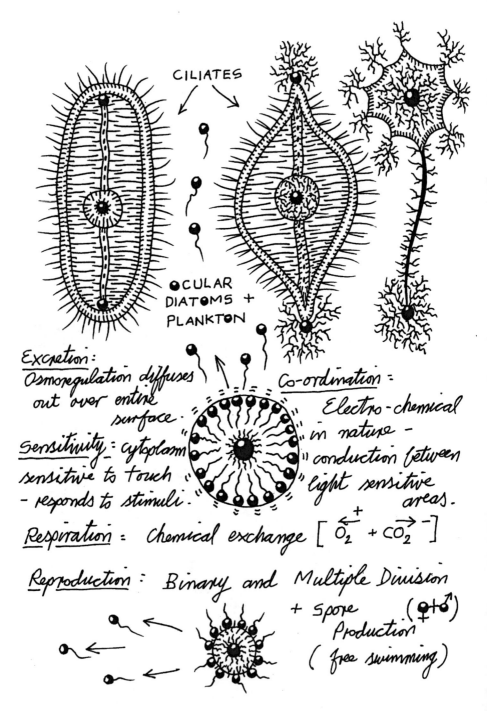

CILIATES

OCULAR
DIATOMS +
PLANKTON

Excretion:
Osmoregulation diffuses
out over entire
surface.

Sensitivity: cytoplasm
sensitive to touch
- responds to stimuli.

Co-ordination :
Electro-chemical
in nature -
conduction between
light sensitive
areas.

Respiration = Chemical exchange $[\overset{+}{\overleftarrow{O_2}} + \overset{-}{\overrightarrow{CO_2}}]$

Reproduction : Binary and Multiple Division
+ Spore ($♀$+$♂$)
Production
(free swimming)

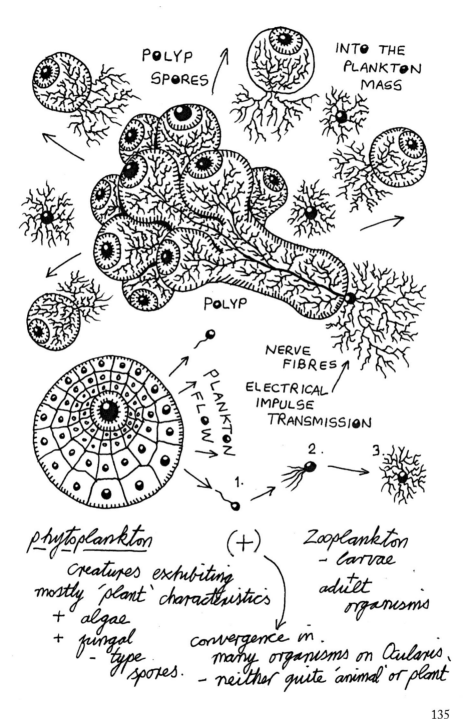

POLYP
SPORES

INTO THE
PLANKTON
MASS

POLYP

NERVE
FIBRES

ELECTRICAL
IMPULSE
TRANSMISSION

PLANKTON
FLOW

1.
2.
3.

phytoplankton

(+)

Zooplankton
- larvae
+
adult
organisms

creatures exhibiting
mostly 'plant' characteristics
+ algae
+ fungal
- type
spores.

convergence in.
many organisms on Ocularis.
- neither quite 'animal' or plant

135

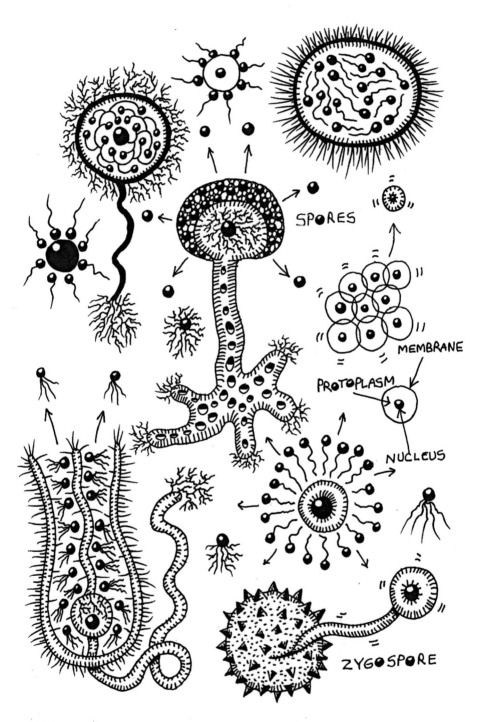

SPORES

MEMBRANE

PROTOPLASM

NUCLEUS

ZYGOSPORE

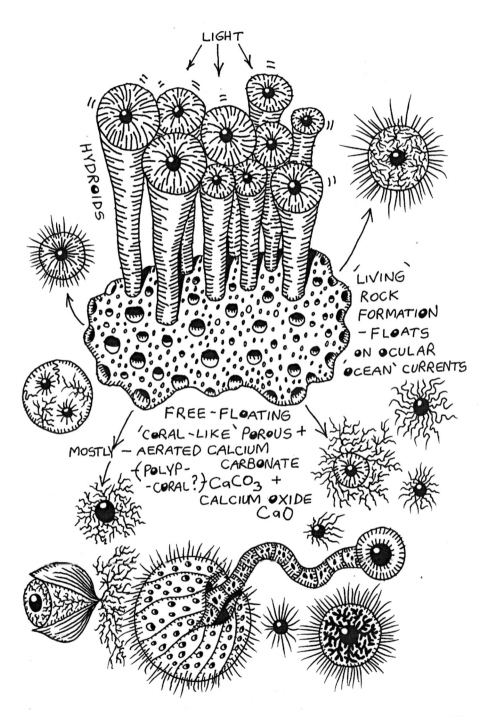

LIGHT

HYDROIDS

'LIVING'
ROCK
FORMATION
— FLOATS
ON OCULAR
'OCEAN' CURRENTS

FREE-FLOATING
'CORAL-LIKE' POROUS +
MOSTLY — AERATED CALCIUM
$\{$ POLYP-   CARBONATE
-CORAL?$\}$ $CaCO_3$ +
CALCIUM OXIDE
CaO

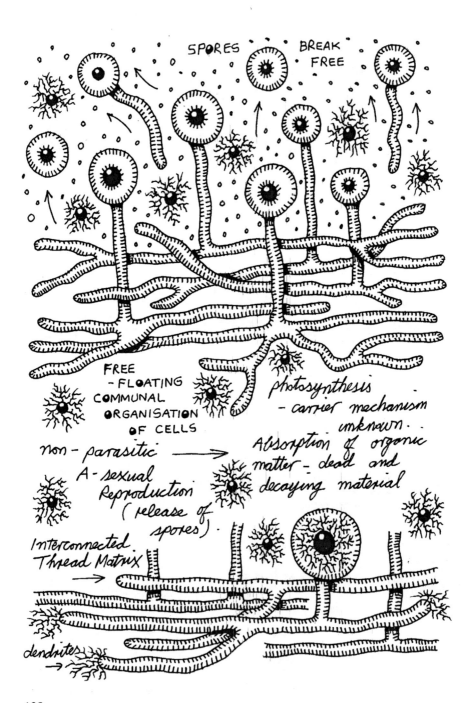

SPORES   BREAK
FREE

FREE
- FLOATING
COMMUNAL
ORGANISATION
OF CELLS

photosynthesis
- carrier mechanism
unknown.

non - parasitic ⟶

A - sexual
Reproduction
(release of
spores).

Absorption of organic
matter - dead and
decaying material

Interconnected.
Thread Matrix
⟶

dendrites
⟶

138

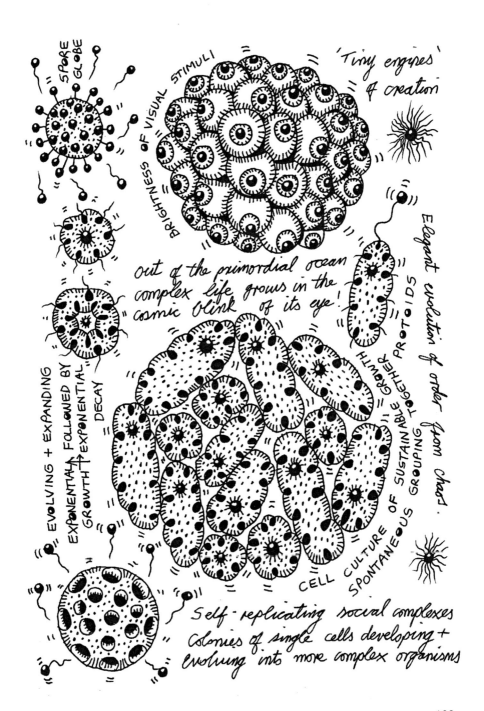

SPORE GLOBE

BRIGHTNESS OF VISUAL STIMULI

'Tiny engines' of creation

out of the primordial ocean complex life grows in the cosmic blink of its eye!

Elegant evolution of order from chaos.

GROUPING TOGETHER PROTOIDS

CELL CULTURE OF SUSTAINABLE GROWTH

SPONTANEOUS GROUPING TOGETHER

EVOLVING + EXPANDING

EXPONENTIAL GROWTH FOLLOWED BY EXPONENTIAL DECAY

Self-replicating social complexes Colonies of single cells developing + evolving into more complex organisms

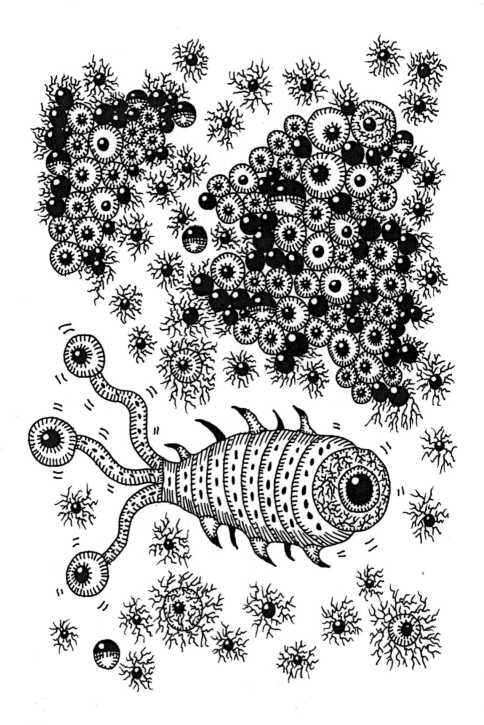

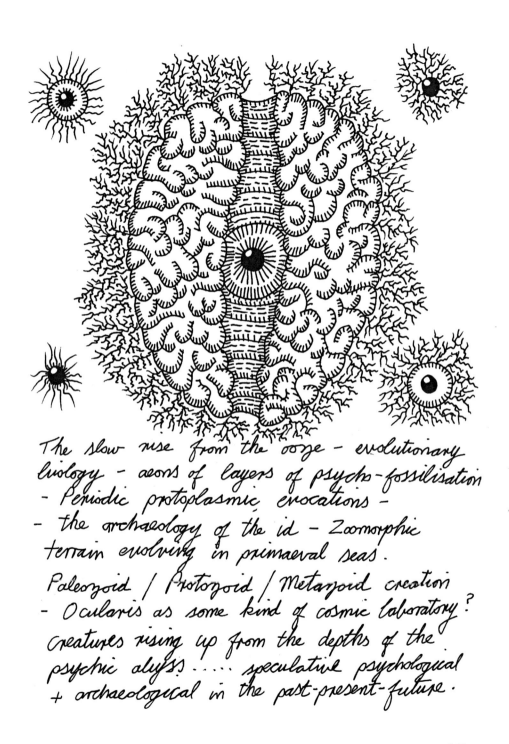

The slow rise from the ooze — evolutionary
biology — aeons of layers of psycho-fossilisation
— Periodic protoplasmic evocations —
— the archaeology of the id — Zoomorphic
terrain evolving in primaeval seas.

Paleozoid / Protozoid / Metazoid creation
— Ocularis as some kind of cosmic laboratory?
creatures rising up from the depths of the
psychic abyss ..... speculative psychological
+ archaeological in the past-present-future.

SPIROID COIL WORM #1.

SPIROIDAL VARIANT #2.

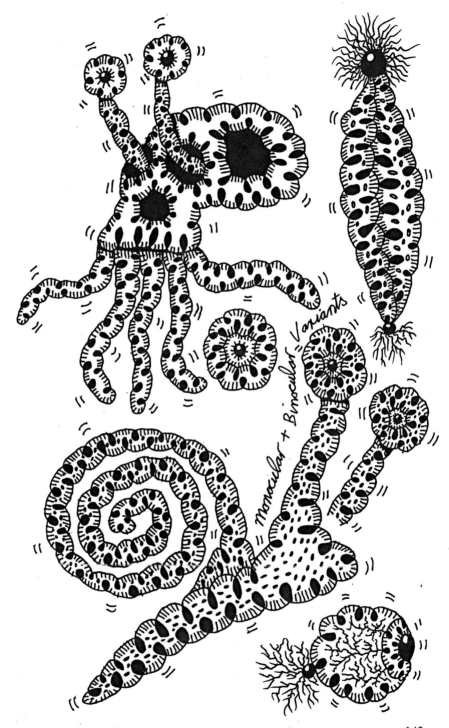

Monocular + Binocular Variants

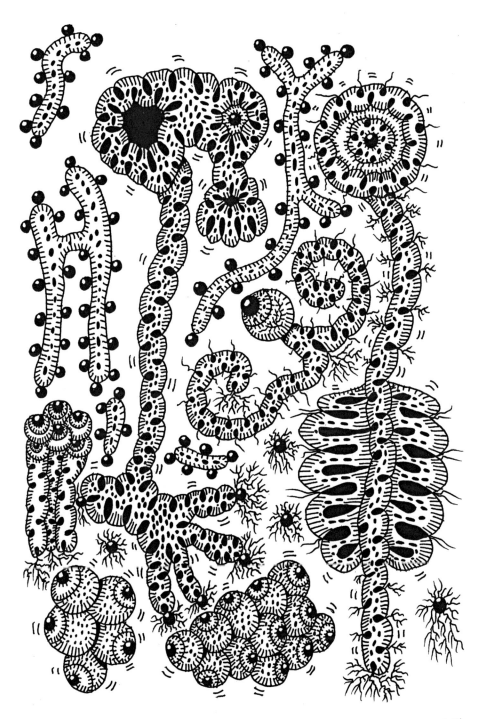

145

146

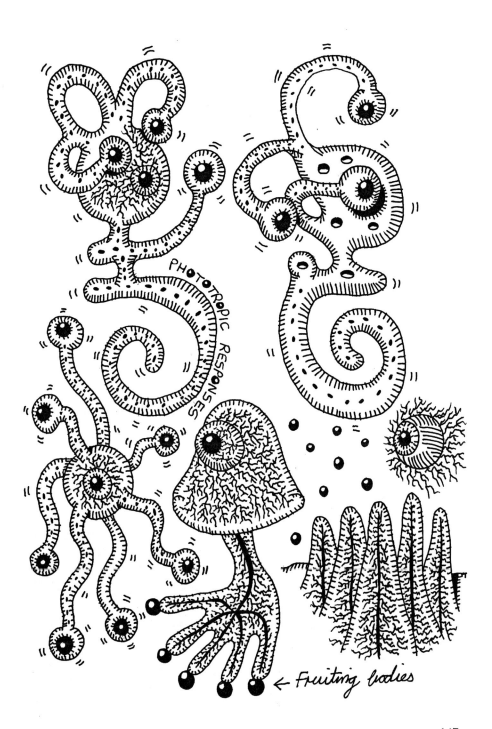

PHOTOTROPIC RESPONSES

← Fruiting bodies

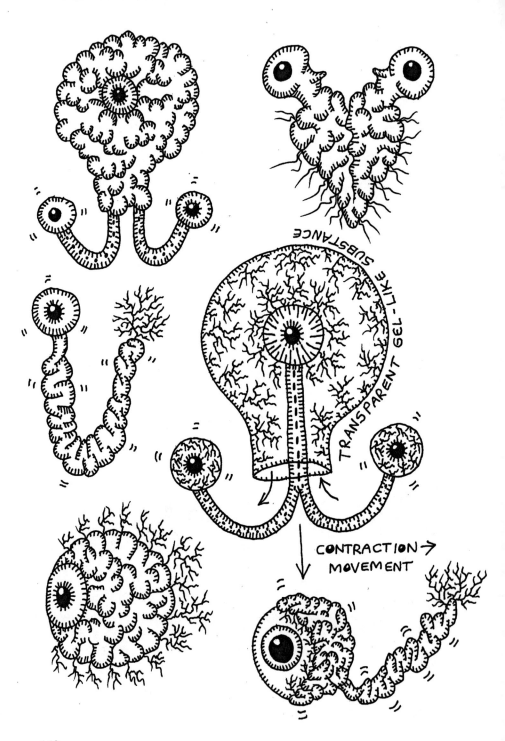

TRANSPARENT GEL-LIKE SUBSTANCE

CONTRACTION→
MOVEMENT

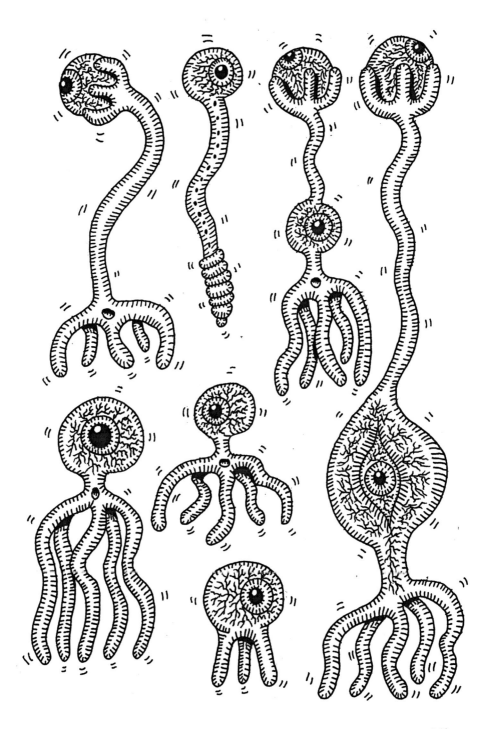

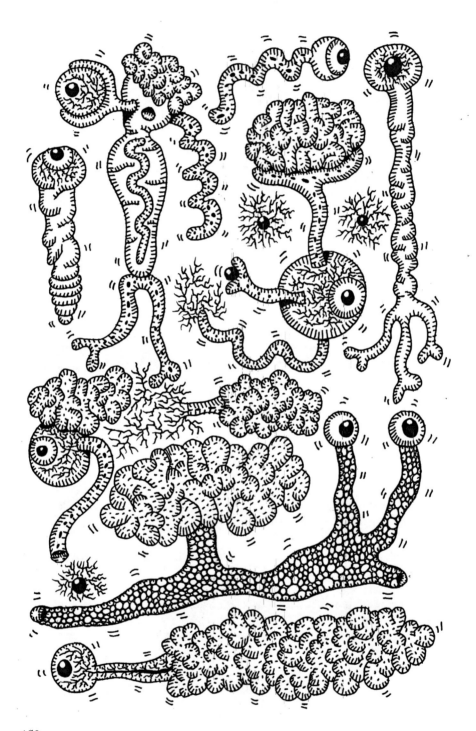

150

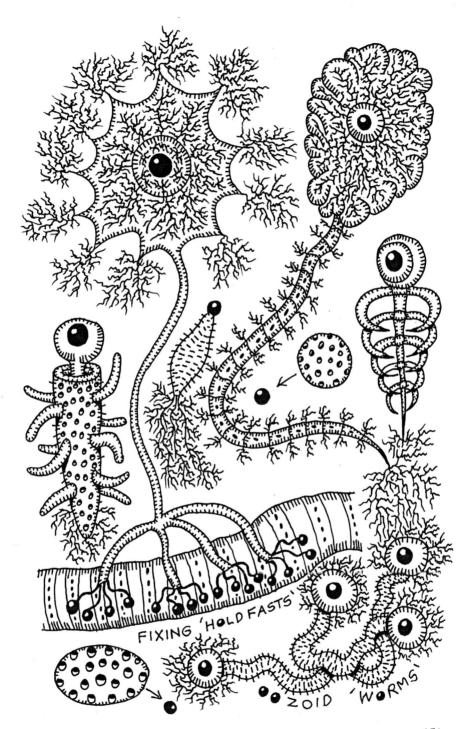

FIXING 'HOLD FASTS'

ZOID 'WORMS'

151

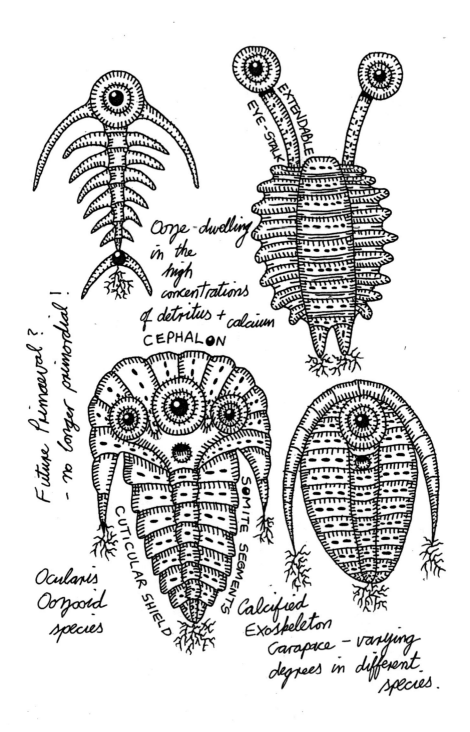

Ooze-dwelling in the high concentrations of detritus + calcium

CEPHALON

EXTENDABLE EYE-STALK

SOMITE SEGMENTS

CUTICULAR SHIELD

Future Primaeval ? - no longer primordial !

Ocularis Oozooid species

Calcified Exoskeleton Carapace - varying degrees in different species.

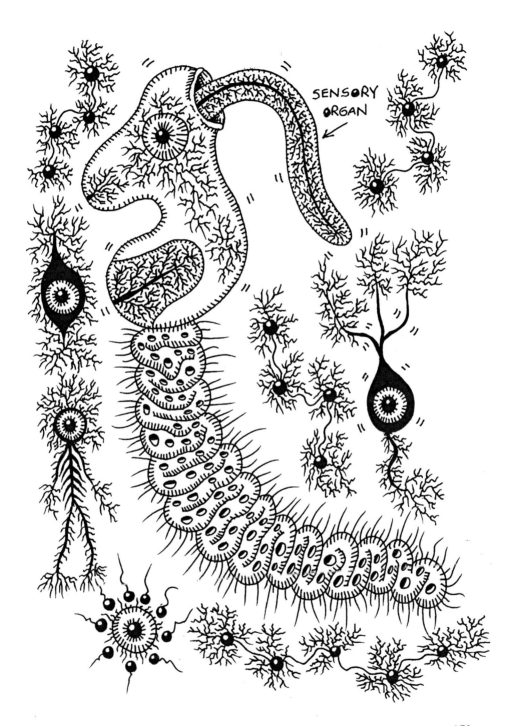

SENSORY ORGAN

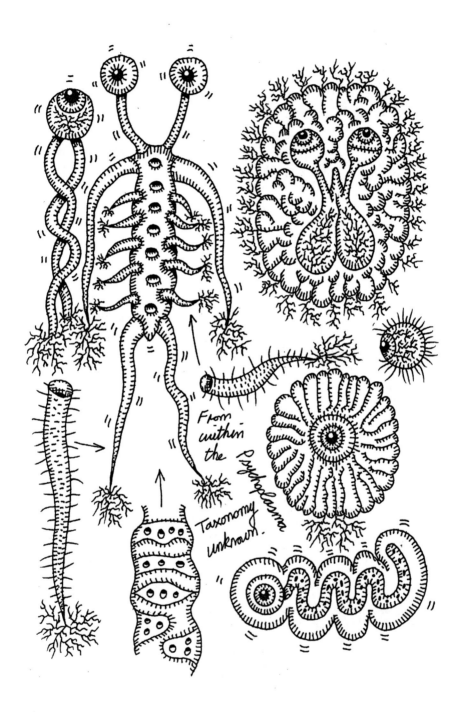

154

In the beginning God created the heavens and Ocularis was without form and void; and darkness was upon the face of the deep. And the spirit of God moved upon the face of the waters.

The Bible, Genesis 1:13
alternative 'cosmic' version

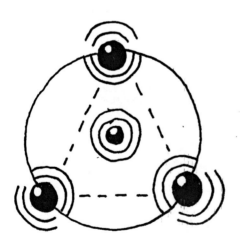

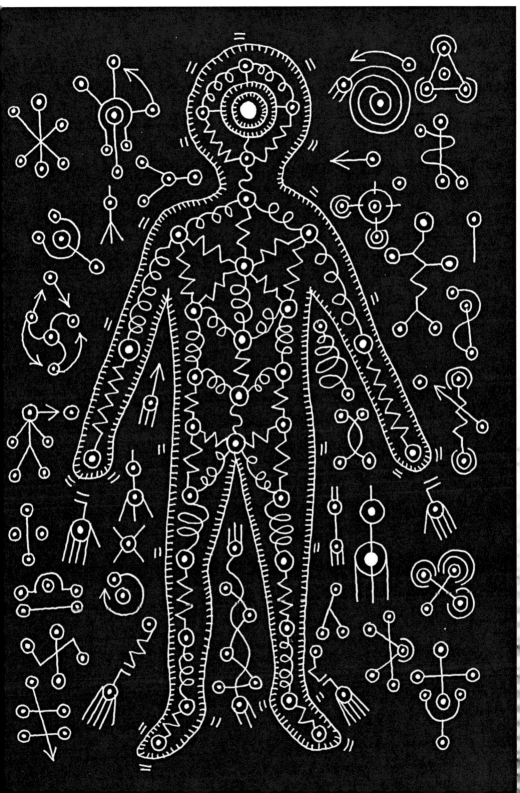

CPSIA information can be obtained
at www.ICGtesting.com
Printed in the USA
FSOW01n0026180216
17020FS